Daddy's House

BY AZAREL

A Life Changing Book in conjunction with Power Play Media
Published by Life Changing Books
P.O. Box 423 Brandywine, MD 20613

Library of Congress Cataloging-in-Publication Data: 2007939105

www.lifechangingbooks.net

ISBN - (10) 1-934230-91-X (13) 978-1-934230-91-6
Copyright ® 2007

Also by Azarel

**BRUISED
& BRUISED 2**

Acknowledgements

Wow! As Mary J. would say, "I'm Going Down!"

I never thought I'd make it through this one. Daddy's House has been by far a difficult task. Between juggling my CEO duties at Life Changing Books and writing a book- by the grace of God-I made it! My Heavenly Father always makes it possible for me to succeed. Without Him I would be nothing! Thank You.

A special thanks must go out to my family before I continue. To my husband Tony, I know I drive you crazy. Thanks for standing by me through the late nights, long trips out of town, and books invading our house. I keep telling you all this will end soon-I just can't see the end of the tunnel yet. To my girls, who watch my every move- thanks for being patient. I'll do better with changing up our schedule- I think it's funny how everyday you expect to go to the post office, UPS, then to the bank. I love you both. Iman, that ATM card is coming!

I am so blessed to have a slew of family members who stick with me consistently in life. Mommy and Bill, thanks for always being there. Daddy and Joyce,

I'm so thankful for your support. To my two grandmothers, Lover and Gram, I can't imagine what my world would be like without the two of you. And to my grandfather Toot, know that I am here for you. To my sister Tam, I love you dearly. Thanks for being there whenever I need you. You continue to wear many hats…now you got that hush thing going (www.boutiquehush.com). I better rock a new bag every week. Kinae, what can I say? You are a little me in training. Stay off the phone! Love ya!

A special shout out to the LCB Board; Don, Jeremiah, Bean, Tamara, and Anthony. Shout out to the Fenners, Cookes, Williams, Newells, Vicks, Kinneys, Fords, Freemans and the Greens. I love you all. Also, to my dearest cousin, Candice. You told me to make sure I put you in the acknowledgements, so I went a step further and wrote this book about you (smile).

To my extended family and circle of friends; I could not write books successfully without your support. There are far too many to name. But let me try to do my best: Leslie German; each and every time we have a deadline, you come through. You may not be able to function after a job; but you handle your business. I thank you from the bottom of my heart. Cheryl and Emily, we've known each other for over twenty years, you both are like sisters to me-love you for life. Danielle Adams, girl we are getting old-you know what we gotta do (smile). Darren Coleman, I gotta crack the whip on you. You have abandoned the whole family-we gotta put you in check. Lisa Williams, even though you're a 'rock star' now, you still mange to support me because you gotta run those books out there! If I hadn't mentioned your name, you know I always leave space for you. Write your name here_____ you know I love you!

To the ladies who hold it down daily at LCB, I don't know how to thank you. You all make it possible for us to do what we do- shine! Leslie Allen, you are Osama bin Laden in a dress. You keep us all on point, and I love you for that. You've been with me since day one- through the good and the bad. You wear many, many hats and can't be thanked enough for all you do. Keep riding us- we need the pressure. Davida Baldwin, I'm so grateful to have you on our team-you are probably the kindest of us all. Your loyalty shows and is appreciated. Keep banging out those hot covers. Nakea Murry, you are the beast in the industry. You know your stuff well, and seem to bring the professionalism needed to succeed, yet you can be crazy when we need you to be (party girl-smile). Thanks for being in my corner. Kathleen Jackson, I thank you for always being there when I need you.

A special thanks goes out to the distributors and vendors who got my back. Hakim, Balde, Gordon, Harris, Sidi, Henry, Nelson, D.C. Bookman, and Lloyd. Know that I appreciate your business and level of respect that comes along with this crazy business. To Kwame and Karen, I appreciate all you've done for me. To my Karibu family, thanks for being in my corner, I wish you all much success. Nati, you are what this business should be about-integrity. You should teach a class and invite you know who. Thanks for being an honorable black brother. To Diane and Ms. Emilyn at Mejah Books in Delaware, thanks for supporting me and lending me your ear when in need.

Mr. Evans at Expressions, thanks for keeping me in check. To my authors: Tyrone Wallace, J. Tremble, Tonya Ridley, Tiphani, Ericka Williams, Nisaa A. Showell, Mike Warren, Mike G, Danette Majette, Sheree Avent, Marissa Monteilh and Carla Pennington, thanks for being apart of the LCB family. Let's kill 'em in 2008. Thanks to the Flexin' and Sexin' family, Kwan, Anna J., Eric S. Gray, Juicy Wright, Brittani Williams and Aretha Temple. You guys put out the hottest anthology ever.

A special shot out to the people who always keep LCB events in place; Antonio Carver, Keisha George and Reshaun Brent. Your help and support is greatly appreciated.

To those of you who know me well, you know my desire to give to those in need. Please go to Spreading Literacy and Love www.spreadlitandlove.com and help me change the lives of our underprivileged youth.

Again, to those of you not mentioned, it's been a rough year for me, so please know that it's my mind and not my heart.

Peace,

Azarel

Chapter One

The unusual sound outside my low budget apartment scared me once again. I opened my left eye slightly, only to see that my bedroom door was still locked and securely in place. I clearly remember the maintenance man clowning me when I paid him extra money to come by and install the double bolt on the inside of my bedroom door. He thought my cautious nature was over the top, and laughed at me, saying the neighborhood wasn't that bad. Little did he know, I'd gone up against worst things in my life than just a few neighborhood criminals. Hell, maybe the maintenance man was crooked too, 'cause I'd been taught to trust no one.

As usual, my hallucinating antics had gotten the best of me. I wanted to get up and double check the noises that I was sure came from outside, but my body lay stuck like it had been glued to the bed. I had just finished another twelve hour shift at Texaco, and wanted to sleep my ass off. Although I'd tossed and turned for hours, the rattling sounds became clearer. *Four o'clock*, I thought, *nobody should be out and about at this hour*. I lifted my head for a quick second and stared at the clock again, just to verify there were only three more hours before my ass needed to clock back in for work. I closed my eyes tightly, determined to get what sleep I could.

Despite all that had gone on over the past year, I managed to fall back into a light sleep. After all, this was the safest place the feds had found for me so far. The one bedroom garden apartment was a far cry from my last residence in Flint, Michigan, where drug dealers and pimps lived only two blocks away. It reminded me of Brooklyn, where I was born and raised, and where my life was ruined.

Normally, the witness protection program only offered *some* financial assistance to start you off and *some* employment, but I was classified under special services as *needy*, a nut case is what they really thought. Eight months ago, I started my first day in the program, and nothing had worked until this place outside of Hamilton, New Jersey came along.

It was a decent spot, but I still couldn't figure out why the feds would put me so close to New York City, where everything originally went down. I mean, I'd been sent clear across the country, and now I was only two and a half hours away from the place that got me in this situation.

As I slipped into what I thought was a deep sleep, I could still hear my mother calling me the day she was arrested; the day we were *all* arrested. "Candice! Candice!" I thought I heard her say. I frowned and twitched under my sheets at the sound of her raspy voice, but was determined to ignore it. I desperately needed some uninterrupted sleep.

I sunk deeper into the covers, and pulled my knees closer to my stomach. I had almost found that perfect position, until the crashing noise of my front door being ripped off its hinges, scared the shit out of me.

Instinct kicked in. I jumped up trying to remember what I was supposed to do. My escape route had been planned and practiced from the first day I moved in. I knew there would come a time when I'd have to run. She wouldn't let me testify alive; she told me to my face. I remember it like it was yesterday. My own mother really wanted me dead. The rambling and thrashing sounds told me they were trashing my living room. My heart must've stopped. All I heard were the words, "She's in there," someone said, as they continued to bang.

The voices were deep, muffled, and unfamiliar. From what I understood, my mother, Velma 'Big V' Holmes was still locked down, and would be until the trial. Unfortunately for me, she was like God—*there even when I couldn't see her*.

Her connections were strong, even in Jersey. Once, these three armed men ran up in her stash house, unloading round for round. Their aim was to knock off everybody in her operation. My uncle said it was like a scene out of an Italian mafia movie. Big V, not only walked toward the bullets, she was somehow able to grab one of the assailants and shoot him dead in the face, blowing off his nose. Always prepared, he said that after her sniper rifle was empty, she exposed a revolver, finishing off the job. My baby Rich told me he was the only one who didn't run. Everybody else fled after shooting a few rounds. Still in all, Big V and Rich finished the job. I heard my mother never flinched.

The crazy part was that all this went down at an illegal stash house, but somehow, even after the bodies were taken out and the news reporters publicly aired her dirty laundry, she still managed to beat the charges. She got off because the property was in her name, and the assailants entered illegally, with the intent to harm her. Not only that, she dealt with her workers who didn't stand strong.

We all knew it was bullshit, but her money was long, and her talk-game was right. So, as far as I knew, she could be out on bail right now. *Damn, if this is what she meant by bringing in the heavy artillery, she meant business,* I thought.

"Bitch, you dead!" one of the voices shouted, from the other side of my bedroom door. His raging voice brought me back to reality.

Twenty seconds passed and I was still in my bed, scared to move.

"Where da fuck you hidin'!" one of the voices shouted in between more smashing sounds. Shit, shit, shit, what the hell am I going to do? I panicked even more. Fear took hold of my thoughts. I inched back in the corner of my bed pulling my covers with me. For some reason I thought if I'd shielded myself, they wouldn't be able to get into the room. The hard rattling and powerful shaking of the knob made me wet myself a little. I wanted to yell back just to see if my mother was on the other side, but decided against it. I also wondered if my old love, Rich was out there too. He claimed to love me, but Big V had probably convinced him that I was the enemy. Hell, for all I knew she could've been screwing him. That's how she got down. She did anything to stay at the top of her game and keep her crew loyal. Unfortunately, she and Rich were two of a kind-ruthless. So if he was after me, I would be yesterday's trash.

Boom! I felt the vibration of someone's body hit the door. I sat up in attention. My heart raced so fast it skipped beats. I couldn't catch my breath. Okay move dumb ass, I whispered inside. But for some reason my body still didn't respond. Sweat poured down the center of my back.

"Make sure you cut that hoe's neck straight across the center," I heard one of the intruders say to another.

"Bitch where you at?" one yelled, while they continued to ram into my door. I heard my ceramic plant vases hit the walls. Glass shattered. I wondered how many were out there. Those guys obviously meant business the way they rummaged through my apartment.

Bam! They kicked hard enough for the top hinge to break off my bedroom door. Oh my God! I leaped from the bed getting my feet tangled up in the sheets. I fell flat on my face.

"We gon' rape your ass?" one of them whispered through the slight opening at the top of the door. It was almost like he could see me. I kicked the air trying to break free. As I squirmed, I scrambled to grab my shoes from near the dresser, but my arms were too short to reach them.

"Oh bitch, you mine now," the one with the deeper voice yelled, as he peeled the first hinge from the door.

I wanted to cry but I had no time to get into my emotions. It was do or die. As I freed my left foot, I slid across the floor like a soldier in combat. My closet seemed so far away.

My aim was to retrieve my purse with my life savings and my identification, then head straight for the window. When I reached the closet I stood to my feet. I felt around in the dark like a blind woman without her cane.

Bam! I watched as the second hinge separated. Oh shit…shit…shit! I began to throw my clothes on the floor when I couldn't find the hook with my purses.

"Run bitch run, 'cause we coming to get yo' ass!" The man squeezed his arm through the slight opening of the door, and shined the red laser from what appeared to be his gun. *Please don't let them kill me.*

Finally, I felt the metal beads on the handle of my fake Prada bag. I yanked the long strap, threw it across my shoulder, and darted toward the window. Within that one second, shots rang out. I ducked praying that the bullets would go around me and under me, but not through me. I pulled the thick curtain aside to escape. I don't know why I looked back, but I did. I could see in the shadow two big bodies, one headed straight in my direction. I wrestled with the window as the bullets kept coming. One hit the window and glass went everywhere. What the hell!

Just when I raised the window, even though it was already broken, the one headed for me grabbed my top. I tussled to get loose banging my head on the frame.

"Bitch you dead!" His voice sent chills down my spine.

He put the gun to my head. I'm dead! I thought. I almost surrendered until he pulled the trigger. Click, click, click. It was empty. He had already unloaded all his rounds. I guess his ass was in shock 'cause he let me go, holding it in his hands like it was his baby. I was in disbelief. Everything at that point seemed to have happened in slow motion. Move dummy, I said to myself.

The dangling of my leg from the window ceil snapped me back to reality. As planned, I squeezed my petite body through the window and out into the cold. Being outside in the middle of the night in a silk Victoria Secret pajama set was not a part of the plan, but in this game, anything goes. The moment my bare feet touched the fire escape, my nipples jumped to attention. The brisk air had me jilted, but I instantly slipped into survival mode.

My heart raced. I wanted to cry out for help, but who would save me? If the police came, they'd just put me in another place until it was time for the trial, and I'd just be a sitting target all over again.

I picked up the pace, fearing for my life. Luckily, the temperature had gotten up to about fifty degrees, and wasn't too unbearable for me to be out without a coat. By the time I swung from the last step of the fire escape to the street level, I'd already figured out that I had nowhere to go. I hesitated, swaying back and forth, contemplating which way to run. *Damn, I wish I had a pair of socks or something in this purse.*

Suddenly, the gun shots from above let me know they'd finally reloaded their gun. I turned to see if I was being watched. In the distance, I saw a big black gruesome-looking dude with his head stuck out of my window. By the way his head turned, I could tell he was searching hard to find me. I could see another large shadow hovering behind him.

I slid closely alongside the wall, trying to stay far away from the street lights. I glided smoothly down the street like an Olympic ice skater, never looking back. Just when I thought I had made it scot-free, Big Foot spotted me. "Oh, we gon' get yo muthufuckin' ass, cunt!" he roared. His voice resonated so loudly, more lights began to come on all over the building. "Run bitch, run!"

By the time he finished his last words, I'd already taken his threatening advice. I darted like a run away slave, from what was supposed to have been a safe haven. I'd finally made it to the end of my street. Between sprinting and looking around, trying to watch my back, I tripped twice, scraping my knees. The further away I ran, the streets became darker and colder, but I continued to sprint with the fastest speed possible.

The first few blocks were the hardest, because everything around me appeared to be a threat. Even the mailboxes had eyes. I felt like they were watching me too. I wondered who would help me on a night like this. I had no one. I thought about going to a shelter, but the further I traveled, I realized the neighborhood had become more suburban. I was surrounded by nothing but houses. I'd walked nearly four miles and my feet felt beat up by the cold concrete.

Out of breath, I finally slowed down, after realizing the coast was clear. I grabbed my forearms tightly, noticing how the neighborhood had changed drastically. The upscale homes reminded me of the type of lifestyle I wanted to live some day.

Between my wishful thinking, and the eagerness to be saved, I zoned out. The sudden screeching sound of a zooming car brought me back to the present. The bright lights glared in my face, and sent me back into escape mode. I panicked and jetted through someone's backyard. I didn't care if the car was coming for me or not. I just wasn't willing to take that chance.

My eyes bulged when I spotted a oversized three foot doghouse sitting in the back of someone's yard. For most, that was a sign that a big dog would be waiting to tear their ass up. But I had nothing to fear, I had a way with animals. Big V kept vicious pit bulls around, so I learned how to make them submit real easily. Besides, my only choice was Big Velma's hit men or Foo-Fee, Foo-Fee. I decided on the dog.

I unzipped my purse, searching for anything to protect me from a possible upcoming attack. Moving closer, I tip-toed alongside the doghouse like a tightrope walker. Still fumbling around in my bag, I dropped closer to the ground, and decided to use the scarf off my head as bait. I waved the scarf back and forth in front of the doghouse. Nothing happened. "Here boy," I whispered, knowing he'd come running. Again, nothing happened. A dog would've definitely smelled my scent by now, and headed for my flesh, so I eased up a bit. A tear fell, starting a chain reaction. I didn't know whether my tears were from not getting bit, or from the reality of my next move.

The moment I got on all fours and crawled into the doghouse, I knew I'd reached my lowest point. Tears flooded my vision when I entered, and pushed my way to the back. The offensive odor hit me like a bowling ball going fifty mph. I gagged a few times, before realizing what was happening to me. In a strange way, getting bit was what I wanted. I needed to be taken from my misery. Just maybe, I'd end up dead.

I tied my scarf back around my head like it was bed-time. The ventilation was poor, damn near unbearable. But at that point, I had no choice but to weather the storm. I crouched in the corner and talked to myself. That kept me sane. Cold and shivering, I finally knew what it felt like to be homeless.

Daddy's House

Chapter Two

The next morning, I was posted up in the doghouse, like I was waiting for a bowl to be placed in front of me. Between scratching all over like a junkie, and trying to blow the bad smell from my nose, I'd completely flipped out. Teary-eyed and hungry, I still didn't wanna move. The thought of being that afraid had me freaked out. The doghouse seemed to be the most unlikely place where anyone would look for me. I just prayed the beast who owned the spot wouldn't be coming home anytime soon.

I looked down at my body, and was instantly reminded that I still had on a pajama set with no shoes, and a flowery stitched scarf. At the thought of my attire, I snatched the scarf off my head, and combed my long jet black hair from its wrap with my fingers. Luckily my texture was good, and a few strokes of my hand made me look decent enough to walk around the neighborhood. I crawled to the edge of the doghouse, and peeped out into the sunlight. The house in front of me didn't look as huge the night before when I decided to trespass, but now it looked humongous. I wondered if the dog was inside, or from the looks of things, at the dog spa. The manicured lawn and top of the line outdoor furniture told me that somebody there had *money*.

At the thought of money, I stuck my head back inside, grabbed my purse, and dumped what little laid inside. All I had to my name was inside my wallet. I counted slowly, hoping I was wrong. "Twenty, forty, sixty, eighty, eighty-one, eighty-two." I knew that wasn't enough for an escape. Obviously whoever came for me last night, knew where I was. So I needed real money to make sure I wasn't found again.

I peeped out once again, and rose to my feet. Without a watch, I could only guess the time. I figured from the look of the sun, 9:00 a.m. was approaching. Boldly, I walked around to the side of the house, past the iron railings, clutching my forearms tightly. The air was brisk, but decent for early November. I knew no one would believe my situation, but it was worth a try.

I rang the doorbell, and lowered my head only to notice my bare feet again. I shook my head, thinking, *I would definitely call the cops if I lived here. What should I say? Should I tell them I think my mother has a hit out on me? Who in the hell would believe me?* I tried to focus on something different, 'cause I knew a breakdown was coming. I turned to admire the beautiful scenery of the leaves changing colors on the trees, but that was just a fairy tale; reality stared me in the face.

"May I help you?" an elderly white woman asked, opening the door just slightly. She looked at me strangely, from my face down to the bottom of my feet. Slowly, her eyes moved like a scanner. "Dear, I hope you're not looking for work," the woman uttered. "Coming here dressed in nightclothes is utterly rude!"

I said nothing, but raised my head a bit.

"Well, say something. What do you want?"

Our eyes locked and so did my brain. "Uhhhhhh...," I stuttered.

"Yes...what do you want?" she repeated.

A tear fell and my face reddened. "My boyfriend put me out in the street," I said sincerely. "Me and my baby have nowhere to go." I started crying openly. I was good at making people feel sorry for me.

"Oh my goodness," the woman said, with her hand placed directly over her chest. Her jaw dropped low. I guess the baby thing did it. She just wasn't smart enough to ask where the baby was. "I saw something like this on the *Montell Williams Show* once. What do you want me to do, dear?" she asked, opening the door just a little bit more.

"Can I come in just for a while?" I asked, with more crocodile tears flowing down my face. "He may be looking for me."

The woman hesitated. She looked over her shoulder, and answered with regret, "Oh honey, I can't do that. My husband would kill me. You would be putting us in danger," she said, like she was dividing every syllable. "I really want to help, believe me. I had a black girl working for me once."

I nodded my head, as if to say sure, then just smiled at her racist-ass.

"Oh, I didn't mean anything by that," she said, as her face turned a deeper red. "Wait at the end of the driveway, down there at the bottom of the hill," she pointed. "I'll give you a few dollars."

The lady started to close the door, when I stuck my foot in the opening of the door, and prayed she wouldn't slam it.

"What in God's name are you doing?" she shouted, pushing the door almost completely shut. Her eyes grew to the size of watermelons, and it became obvious she thought she was being robbed.

I just shook my head, "Can you at least call me a cab?" I asked with begging eyes, through the tiny slit left in the door.

She looked hesitant again, but agreed. "Wait at the bottom of the hill," she instructed again skeptically, and watched my every move. The moment she shut the door, I heard about four deadbolts being locked one after another.

I turned and walked away pitifully. All my life I'd been let down, so this was no different. I don't know why I thought a complete stranger would go out of her way for me, when not one person in my family cared at all, other than my cousin, Tracey. As a matter of fact, they all probably wanted me dead; my mother, uncles, aunts and cousins. I was starting to think that I deserved it.

I slowly walked down to the bottom of the driveway, wondering if she would keep her promise. Then I thought about my other option, call Agent Barnes. He would surely have me picked up in no time, and placed in another situation with a new identity. For the last few months I'd been Ms. Danielle Crouch instead of my real name, Candice Holmes. *What a name*, I thought. For me, Danielle Crouch was getting old. I needed to make a way on my own, without the help of the system. I was starting to feel like my family was right. Testifying against them probably wasn't the brightest thing to do.

I finally found a secluded area near a bush at the bottom of the hill, knelt down and waited for my cab. I wondered if the woman had even called. *She may have called the police instead*, I thought. No one could be trusted.

For the next twenty minutes, I contemplated my next move. When Tracey came to mind, I knew it was a bad decision, but the most comfortable one. After all, she was my first cousin, born to my aunt, Vicki, my mother's sister.

Tracey lived in Harlem, and was one of the rebels of the family, who departed ways from our relatives years ago. She was five years older than me, but we'd always been close. Tracey felt like what I did was right. She said she would've done the same damn thing. "Fuck'em all," she said.

I remember using her as my one phone call the night I got locked up. She said I didn't deserve to be in jail, and to do what I had to do. Taking her advice, I did just that. But here I was, twelve months later, all fucked up.

I hadn't talked to Tracey since that night, but had somehow convinced myself in a matter of minutes that I was gonna call to see if I could stay with her for a while.

As my cab approached, the white woman emerged from her house. She pranced down the hill like a letter carrier waving a telegram. I turned my back and waved down the speeding cab. I didn't have anymore time to waste.

"Hey!" she yelled. "Wait!"

I kept walking and hopped into the cab. I didn't wanna face her again. I'd embarrassed myself enough.

The cab driver had already rolled down the back window, and the woman leaned in the car before I could object. "This for you," she said, handing me a white envelope. I hesitated, and just gazed at the envelope. Although it was flat, I figured she only had big bills, and was thankful for her help.

The woman started sniffing like the smell was familiar. I wondered if she realized it was me who smelled like her dog. I lowered my head again in shame.

She placed the envelope in my hand firmly and backed away. "Good luck," she uttered. I guess she felt guilty for the undercover racial insult.

"Let's go," I told the driver.

"Where to?" he asked, in his Asian accent.

"Amtrak." I shot the woman a look that said thank you, as the driver pulled off. She smiled slightly, but I couldn't smile back. Besides, I had nothing to smile about.

The ride was quiet, just what I needed. The cab driver kept looking back at me, probably wondering why I looked like I'd just gotten up. He had no idea I was running for my life, bad breath and all. I made sure I didn't make eye contact, 'cause I didn't want him asking me any questions. I leaned back into the torn leather seat, and cried inside like a baby.

Visions of my mother's mocha-colored face consumed my mind. On the outside, we seemed so much alike, except for our weight. Side by side we would walk, turning the heads of every guy in sight. We were known as the mother and daughter with the bootylicious butts, until hers expanded too much. She grew in size, becoming a full-figured woman, yet still beautiful in the face. People always said my smooth deep brown skin came compliments of my mother. I'd always just smile, because good looks and deep dimples were the only things she'd ever given me.

For some reason, she thought employing me within her empire was a gift. Instead, it was a curse. Whenever I felt pain, I thought of her. Whenever I felt afraid, I thought of her too. Strangely, most of the time she was the one putting fear into my heart. Fear was nothing to Big V. Although we were only thirteen years apart, she took control of the streets like she'd been around for years. She had our ruthless neighborhood on lock ever since I was twelve. Of course, she claimed it was all for me. "We gotta eat," she'd say. "I gotta take care of my girl. You ain't got no damn daddy."

I remember her getting her big break five years ago when I turned seventeen. She hooked up with Luther, a Columbian who had major paper. Luther started fronting my mother drugs, and told her all she had to do was get the customers and keep'em satisfied. Big V did just that. She locked down the streets by any means necessary. She surrounded herself with notorious killers, who handled all her dirty work, and made a name for herself. She committed murders, shot up blocks, paid off cops, and screwed whoever she had to in order to get to the top. That was her specialty, my mother claimed to love everyone she ever met. That was her way of bamboozling her way to the top.

For years, my mother brainwashed me into thinking that she really loved me too and that putting in work for her would be short-lived. She lied for years, saying that I would be on my way to college as soon as she made her first million. Well, that mil never came. I was just another one of her cash cows.

On my twentieth birthday, I remember asking her if I could finally go to school full time. Her reply was, "Bitch, who needs school? And who gon pay for it? I got crack-heads to invest in!"

For most who knew her, bragged that she was a beast, not to be fucked with, but I was her seed. I figured I'd get cut some slack. I just wanted to be free. I never wanted to be in that life anyway. She warned me to never double cross her, and said if I did that I would surely die. Big V was known to keep promises.

I got teary eyed thinking about how she was my blood, but realized I had to be strong. I'd been taught by Big V to be fearless against others, especially the streets. That just didn't work when it came to her.

The driver's voice brought me back to reality. "Thirty-one fifty," he said, eyeing me through his rearview mirror. We were sitting in front of the station and I hadn't even noticed. I opened my purse to pay, when I thought about the envelope the white woman had given me. I quickly ripped it opened, and stuck my hand inside. My heart fluttered. *She couldn't have.*

"What the fuck!" I shouted.

The driver looked at me like I was crazy. I grabbed the five dollar bill from inside the envelope, and added it to my $82.00 life savings. I couldn't believe the white woman thought five dollars would be helpful. I paid my bill, hopped out, and headed into the Trenton, New Jersey station bold, bare foot and all. Hopefully the driver wasn't too upset that he'd only received a fifty cent tip, but now wasn't the time to be generous. I was on a mission.

Once inside, I stood there looking at the big board, thinking about which way I would go. I got constant, dis-approving stares from the waiting passengers. One man went as far as fixating his eyes on me, and pressing his daughter's face against his pant leg, to keep her from looking at me. He frowned for minutes, like I'd done something to him, but I couldn't worry about that. I had to make moves. I knew my money wouldn't take me far, but I wondered if I had enough to make it any further than two stops.

I couldn't shake the rambling thoughts in my head. I pictured myself contacting Agent Barnes, and him sending a car for me right away. The only problem was when my ride pulled up, my mother was the one driving.

I stood in the station going crazy, until the best idea hit me. I darted to the pay phones in the corner near the snack shop. The quarters went in slowly, and I prayed the call wasn't a mistake. Tracey's number hadn't changed in over ten years, so it was easy to remember. She answered on the first ring.

"Who da fuck is this callin' me so early?" she asked.

I hesitated at the thought of how hood she was. Maybe her place wasn't gonna be the best move for me. I had my bout with the hood life.

"Who da fuck is playin' on my phone?" she smacked.

"It...itt....itt's...it's me," I finally said.

"Candice?"

"Yeah, it's me, Tracey," I replied slowly.

Her voice changed suddenly. She seemed excited. "Gurllllll, I miss yo ass. They tell me you got out. Where you at?"

I hesitated again. "Have you heard from my mother?"

"Hell to da naw," she answered quickly. "Last I heard that trick was still locked down, probably intimidating somebody's daughter by now." She laughed. "Besides, the whore told me a year ago that she hated me, and if I wasn't her niece she would'a had me gutted like a pig for runnin' my mouth. So fuck her!" Tracey let out another one of her crazy, loud laughs.

"Look, girl, I'm in trouble," I confessed.

"Ah-huh," she said, smacking her lips for the second time. "I figured that. Shiiiiiiii…d, that's the only time you call. The last time was a year ago when you first got locked up."

"Seriously, Tracey, some dudes came looking for me and knocked down my door. Big V probably sent'em. I need a place to hang out."

"Where you at?" she repeated.

"Don't worry about that. Can I come stay at your spot for a while?" I looked around nervously making sure I wasn't being watched.

"Sure, but you might as well know, a bitch gotta work to live up in here! If you still as pretty as you used to be, I can get you a few gigs workin' wit' me."

"I ain't into that," I replied. Tracey was still stripping last I knew. "Look, we'll talk later. I'm on my way."

"Wait, what time you gon' get here."

"Ahhh…not sure. Just meet me."

"Where, bitch?"

"Hold on a sec, let me check the time," I said, stretching the phone cord to get a better look at the board listing all the train routes. "Damn!" I shouted. "It leaves in ten minutes. I gotta go. Meet me at Penn Station by Macy's on the 7th Avenue side in a hour. If I don't make the train, I'll call you back. "

"Bet," was all I heard her say before she hung up.

I darted down the stairs, taking two at a time to Track #9. I figured since I had cash, paying on the train would be fine. I breathed a sigh of relief when the train was in sight.

Three steps from the door, a hand flew in my face. "Miss, you can't get on without shoes," a tall guy said. His Amtrak name tag read, Lawrence.

"Looks like you need a man in your life. Didn't your father ever tell you not to walk around without shoes on?"

Damn, I'd never even met my father. My mother told me I was a result of a one night stand.

"But…the train is gonna leave if I go get shoes," I finally responded, damn near out of breath. I gave him the most pitiful look possible. I had to think quickly. "Sir, my boyfriend is after me. He'll kill me if he catches me." I closed my eyes to think about my life. It was the fastest way to make myself cry. Before a tear could fall, the horn blew from the train. There was no time.

I turned to walk away, when Mr. Lawrence yelled, "Go 'head, get on, but watch yourself. The conductor on this train is mean and no-nonsense. You better stick your feet way under the seat, and call the police on that boyfriend of yours," he added.

I hopped on the train, wanting to smile, but just nodded thanks to Mr. Lawrence. Making my way down the aisle, I scanned every seat, trying to choose my spot wisely. Plenty of seats were available, since I'd just missed rush hour. The train started moving, but I was still searching. When I spotted a lady with a baby and a few bags scattered on the floor, I climbed over her to the window seat, thinking it would be the perfect spot to hide my bare feet.

The woman sniffed like she had allergies or something, and then shot me a funny look. I didn't care, getting to safety was more important. I turned my head while she shifted in her seat, and moved her bags back and forth. The moment my eyes looked ahead, I forgot all about the rude woman, and focused on getting my money together for the conductor headed my way. Mr. Lawrence was right, he did have that no-nonsense look. He was tall and bald, and reminded me of Charles Barkely.

As I dug in my purse, scrambling for money, my neighbor hopped up like she couldn't take it any longer, leaving me wide open for the conductor to see. He walked right up to my seat, and hit me with one word. "Ticket," he said sternly. His eyebrows were thick and bushy, and made me scared to even speak.

"I...I...gottta pay cash."

"We don't take cash," he spat.

I looked around to see if there was someone I could give the cash to, so they could just charge my ticket, but no one was seated nearby. I pushed all the money I had left into his face.

"That's not enough!" he fired. "The ticket is $64.00." His scowl sent chills through my spine. He obviously meant business. "You gotta get off at the next stop."

"Noooooooooo...please," I begged. I gripped his pant leg like he was my man leaving me for good.

"Look," he snapped. He turned and lowered his voice. "I normally put people off my train for this kinda shit, but I got somewhere for you to go." He looked from right to left before speaking, "Come with me."

"Where we going?" I asked, following three steps behind. He ignored me and walked straight ahead. He didn't even grab the ticket being held out by the man who was sitting near the end of the car. He just kept moving, bypassing several passengers in the next three cars. Finally, we came to what looked like a maintenance closet, but it read Handicapped Bathroom. I started getting nervous, wondering what I'd gotten myself into.

Before I could think, he pulled my hand, yanked me inside, and locked the door. The sounding of the lock reminded me of my four day stint in jail. The only thing different was that I wasn't locked up this time with Rich, but with this half of a man in front of me.

He unbuckled his belt and looked me dead in the eye, while he spoke. "It's your lucky day today. I'ma save you some money."

"I got $55.00," I pleaded.

"I got something better in mind for you, sweetness." He shot his tongue out like a poisonous rattle snake.

I backed up against the dirty wall, and eyed the growing bulge in his pants. *Damn*, I thought, *I gotta fuck for a train ride?* His grin held power over me. There was no escaping; his oversized body blocked the door knob. I squeezed out half a fake grin, noticing the beads of sweat on his forehead. I made sure I clocked his name tag in case he needed to be identified later.

"Marlin, why are we here?" I asked, letting him know I had one up on him.

He disregarded my question, and placed his left hand forcefully on my shoulder, pushing me toward the ground. I was no stranger to bobbing the knob, but that was when me and Rich were an item. I closed my eyes, thinking of Rich, as my body slid downward. My knees hit the floor of the tight six-by-six bathroom, while my face dodged his rubbery dick. It dangled in front of me momentarily, until he grabbed the back of my head, and shoved his dick against my lips. I purposefully closed my mouth tightly, but his grip proved he wasn't taking no for an answer. Afraid of what might happen, I opened wide, and latched on loosely.

I slobbered and sucked lazily, while tears fell from my face on to my pajama top. Even though I wasn't doing much, he grabbed my head tighter and pressed harder, making me realize my second-rate job still felt good to him. I started making little circles on the head, hoping that it would make him cum fast.

The conductor continued to moan in a light voice, like it was the best head he'd ever gotten. I thought about biting the hell out of him, but then what? Where would I go? I needed to get to Tracey. I closed my eyes, and thought about when Rich used to love me. I reminisced on the times he held me in his arms. In between my thoughts, I could hear his moans getting louder.

"Damn!" he shouted. His breathing got faster and faster, "OOOHHH… YESSSSSSS…"

The more he pushed inside my mouth, the more I cried inside. He began to make crazy movements with his ass. "Damn, girl," he mumbled. When he held out his hand to clutch the wall, I knew the end was near.

Instantly, I started cooperating, which made him make a hissing sound like a satisfied snake. Quickly, I grabbed a hold of his five inches and stroked him faster, like a pro. Pre-cum dripped, and his eyes rolled back into his head as he sung, "Uhhhhhhhhh!"

His voice was loud enough for people to hear, but he didn't care. He moved in and out of my moist, warm mouth quickly, even though his pants straddled just below his knees, holding his legs hostage for extra movement.

Before I knew it, he'd pressed so vigorously, I just knew he was about to hit the back of my tonsils.

"Oh, shiiiiiit!" he shouted, as his breathing resembled a man going into cardiac arrest. He stumbled back, like he couldn't breathe, shoving my head back from his clutch. I prayed he was dying for real.

I wiped the cum from the side of my mouth. Finally his dick went limp right before me. Within seconds, he pushed his dirty dick back into his pants, and walked out like nothing ever happened. No wiping off, no thank you, and no goodbyes.

Even though his conversation wasn't wanted, it would've made me feel better to hear him say something. Getting myself together, I got off the floor and dried my tears. Minutes later, I found my way to the front car, and curled up in a seat like an embarrassed, cheap prostitute. If I hadn't betrayed my old crew, I'd surely have him killed the second his shift ended.

By the time the train pulled into Penn Station, I felt like a sure candidate for the crazy house. I couldn't believe I was actually getting ready to enter the big bad world of New York, looking and smelling like last week's trash.

I pushed past the people exiting the train, only to run dead into Marlin again. He was standing outside the tracks with a policeman in uniform. They had obviously been talking about me, 'cause when I looked like I was gonna go the other way, the police officer motioned for me to come toward him with his finger. He and Marlin were standing side by side and I was scared as hell.

"You tryna skip out?" the officer said, in an unfriendly tone.

"What do you mean?" I asked, in shock.

"You told this man you were gonna pay him, but hid in the bathroom, huh?"

If my eyes could've stabbed the conductor, he would've been dead. "No, sir." I shook my head from right to left continuously, like my batteries were stuck.

"Pay, or go to jail," Marlin said, with a slight grin.

I dug deep into my purse, crumbled up the last of my money and slid it into his hands.

Marlin didn't even count it. He probably didn't care that it wasn't enough. He nodded to the officer a sign that said my debt was paid, and then I was excused.

I rushed up the stairs into the busy station, without looking back. With every tear left in my body falling, I wondered how the world could be so cruel. Why I was even born?

Chapter Three

"Velma Holmes, Visit!" a tall, slender C.O. yelled at me.

"Rude bastard," I mouthed, as I moved in his direction. I cut his ass in two with my eyes. "That's Miss Holmes to you." I shot him my, *fuck you nigga* glare, and blew his dumb-ass what he thought was a kiss, but it was a death wish. *Chop sui, nigga! Chop mufuckin' sui,* I thought.

I knew the visit was from my lawyer. His two-bit-ass had me in this shit hole way too long. Three hundred twenty-two days to be exact. I was tired of hearing 'bout all his empty promises, 'bout how I would be out in a matter of days. Shit, days turned to weeks and weeks turned to months. What the fuck? My daughter, Candice been out! *Today is lynchin' day for his ass.* I was tired of this damn jumpsuit, eatin' the slop they called food, and lookin' at the same ol' walls day in and day out. The lack of sunlight wasn't good for my complexion. Only good thing 'round here were the dykes.

My girl, C.O. Carter, had hooked me up wit' a freaky cell mate, who was doin' that Verizon thang. Not only was she lickin' my pussy every night after nine, but on the weekends too. Boo lovin' definitely had its benefits.

The moment I hit the hallway toward the visitin' room, all the inmates started sweatin' me like I was Beyonce or some shit. I'd become the jailhouse celebrity. But I had every right to it. After all, I was Queen B.

"Whaz up, Big V?" one of my pressed flunkies yelled, from across the room. I gave that bitch the middle finger.

A C.O. walkin' in the opposite direction, shot me a look that said, *don't say shit*. But that didn't intimidate me. I just stared at her like she was next in line for a beat down.

It took a second for the officers to prepare a private room for me and Mr. Stupid Ass. I watched him through the glass fumbling papers, and sweatin' like a fat kid who'd misplaced his food.

"Go on in," mumbled the tall C.O.

That was all I needed to hear. "Yo, why the fuck am I still in here?" I shouted, bursting through the door.

My lawyer's eyes darted to the officer. But little did he know, I had these C.O.'s trained. During my visits, didn't none of 'em sleezy bastards say shit. I had 'em trained like circus animals. The C.O. didn't flinch. Three inches taller than me or not, I could easily chump his slinky-ass anyway.

My lawyer's white-ass must've forgot that I was Big V, the hoe that put the "b" in bitch…a legend in the streets. I pulled the steel chair back with my foot. Sat down across from his ass, and watched as he tried to untie his tongue.

"Uh…uh…," he stuttered, "how've you been making out, Velma?"

I stared at him cold, and tossed him a smirk. I leaned

back in my chair, lettin' the legs rock on twos. "What the fuck is your name again?" I asked, in my thick Brooklyn accent. I continued to look him directly in the eye, but he wouldn't meet my stare.

The sound of the squeakin' chair probably fucked with his head. "Cat got your mufuckin' tongue?" I asked.

"Uum…uum." He tried to clear his throat. "You forgot my name?" he asked, adjusting his Rite Aid looking bifocals. He turned away from me, which pissed me off. I pulled my chair closer, then reached my hand under the table, snatched the zipper from his pants, and grabbed his little three-inch dick. I squeezed it until his face turned blue.

"Look, you white piece of shit, I ask the questions. Got it?"

His ass was scared as two straight men going to prison. Nada! He said absolutely nothin'! Ending my point, I rubbed my fingers across his top lip. "Can you smell what shit smells like, 'cause that's what you're full of!"

He fearfully reached for his briefcase and pulled out a worn business card. "Mr. Sorenson," he said trembling.

"Listen up, and listen good, cracker," I growled, rising from my seat. I snatched the card, and threw it like a Frisbee across the room. "A sista been in here way too fuckin' long. My time is up. Or kiss your family good-bye."

I stuck my finger in the middle of his head, leaving a deep dent. I turned to see what the C.O. thought 'bout my behavior, but his head was buried in a magazine, which meant he didn't give a shit. I turned back around, and brought up as much flem as my throat could gather. Hog spit never felt so good. I let every bit go, and it landed right on the corner of Mr. Sorenson's lip.

"That does it," he said, trying to put a little bass in his voice. He wiped the saliva from his mouth, and gave me the evil eye. Mr. Sorenson stood up with more confidence than I'd ever seen him with before.

"Oh, I'm sorry. Let me get that for you." I reached for his tie.

He backed up. "After all I've done for you, this is the thanks I get?" he asked, with his finger pointed toward his face.

"While you home fuckin' your wife every night, I'm in this mufuckin' wastin' away…missin' out on cash!" I threw the table across the room. "You haven't done nothin' as far as I'm concerned. Ten g's, you bastard! Ten g's, is what I paid your thievin' ass. And for what? I'm still here. You see me," I said, turnin' around like I was a high fashion model. I mixed my raspy voice with some bass. I was prepared to catch a rap for this mutherfucka. I meant business. "I belong back on the street!" I said harshly. My words slid off my lips like syrup off a pancake. "You get me outta here, 'cause I got bizness to handle! You wit' me?"

"I…I…just need some, basic information," he finally spoke. "I think I need to turn this case over to somebody with more experience, you know, more aggressive."

"Whatever the fuck it takes, you stutterin' bastard." I started pacing in the small space. "Just remember, I hired you. You're responsible for my fate," I pointed.

His face balled up into a bright red twist. "I assure you, Ms. Holmes. I assure you," he stuttered. "One thing might move this situation more in our favor."

I cut my piercing eyes at him. "Our favor?" I asked.

"Yeah," he trembled, "I've gotta get you outta here, remember?" His smile was plastic. He closed his briefcase and moved slowly toward the door.

I stumped my foot. "How you gon' represent me?" I tripped him when he passed me. All his shit fell out of his briefcase. "Get up, you dumb mufucka." I stood in front of him just to fuck with his ass. He was pitiful as hell. I decided to cut his lil' short, stubby ass some slack. "Whatchu thinking?" I asked.

"The DA's office is willing to cut your time if you give up a few of your people," he replied, scrambling to get his papers.

"Do I look like a mufuckin' snitch to you!" I felt some warm shit runnin' down my spine. Mr. Sorenson made me hot. I banged the cement wall until the C.O. moved closer my way. "Don't let this pretty face fool ya! I'm a soldier! Learned from the best! My respect is all I got."

"Oh no…I only meant give up the one who told the feds all about you."

"My baby girl? Fuck naw. Just 'cause she punked out on me don't mean shit! She ain't snitch! Y'all just tryin' to set us up! Divide our family in two. Yep, that's right, them mufuckas is trying to trick my ass." I nodded my head. "Me and my daughter gon' be tight when I get out. Tell them mufuckas that!"

"Oh, and they want your connect as well," he said, two inches away from my face. "Would you be willing to turn state's evidence on both of them?"

*Did this mufucka not hear what I just said? I'ma kill this…*With clinched teeth, I foamed at the mouth like a pitbull. I tried to spare his ass, but I sacked the lil' white man like a defensive lineman. I choked the shit out of him after he hit the concrete. I grabbed the steel chair lying next to me, and stuck his head between the hole. But I underestimated the C.O. He was quick…too quick. Within seconds, he was all over me, trying to unglue my hands from the legs of the chair, and the steel bar that was lodged in Mr. Sorensen's throat.

I blacked out. I couldn't hear a voice in range. It took seconds, probably minutes, to bring my ass back. "It ain't worth it, baby," I finally heard the C.O. say. He kept looking back and forth toward the door. My guess, he was waiting for backup. I still didn't care. *Dead Man Walking,* was all I wanted.

"Let go of the chair," the C.O. spoke calmly.

We were all on the floor, intertwined like a damn pretzel. The more blood I saw, the more turned on I was. It was like having an orgasm. My heart pounded. Sweat formed all over me. I started to smile from that sweet pleasure of really injuring his dumb-ass. Then laughter set in. I gave in because I wanted to. I released my grip, mad that I didn't get my full pleasure. I wanted his white-ass carried out in black body bag.

I could'a snapped his neck with my bare hands, but I had to play it smart. I had some unfinished business to take care of on the outside. The King Pin drug charges held over my head would be nothing, compared to the book they'd slam on my ass if I killed that dude. I looked around the room, and wondered why the officer hadn't called for backup.

"You too pretty for this," the C.O whispered.

That was it. I surrendered. I lifted my weight off my ex-lawyer, and turned around to be placed in handcuffs.

Mr. Sorensen didn't move. He looked at me through half closed eyes. "Leave me here and you're dead," I whispered, while the C.O. sent a message through his radio. The prison nurse was the first to trample through the door, followed by three other guards. As they ushered my ass out, I had to put on the charm. "So, you really think I'm pretty?" I asked the slim C.O. as the two female officers stared in shock.

The male C.O. said nothing. He never answered, just nervously looked the other way. "Listen Officer Wells," I said, eyeing his nametag, "I just need someone to talk to." I threw him a puppy dog nod, and ignored his co-workers.

I got his ass. Damn, he's cute, I thought. *I could get with a man like him.* I walked back to my cell smiling...no shackles, no handcuffs...and a report from the outside on the way. *Always on top of my game*, I boasted.

Daddy's House

Chapter Four

I turned in small circles inside the train station, realizing I was a little turned around. I searched for the Seventh Avenue exit sign for the third time. When I turned again, I heard someone call my name. My heart instantly skipped a beat.

"Candice, is that you?"

I turned in the direction of the voice.

"Gurl…what the hell you got on?"

I knew it was Tracey. It had been a while since we'd seen each other, but she hadn't changed. Still a thick chick, she reminded me of Adele Givens' character, Tricks from *The Playa's Club*. Though only twenty-eight, Tracey looked as though she'd lived a hard, long life, and her speech confirmed it.

"Bitch, what'da hell you been doin'? Liftin' weights and shit? Look at you, all toned and shit. You still a lil' petite bitch, though. And you still killin' em with dat ass," she said.

She grabbed my arm and twirled me around, studying me like I was gonna be sold on the block. "Damn, Candice, yo shape look good enough to eat, but where the hell are yo shoes, and what happened to yo clothes? And what's that white shit on the side of your mouth? You must've been sleepin' like hell on the train."

I wanted to ask her where the hell her original set of teeth were, because she was laced with four gold teeth shining brightly in the front of her mouth. Instead, I replied, "Long story. Can we get outta here?"

I started leading the way, like I knew where I was going. For some reason, now that I was around Tracey, I felt even more embarrassed than before at my appearance. Tracey had always known me to be real serious about my clothes back when I had money. Whatever was hot, I rocked. And if I was five minutes late on it, Rich would already have it waiting for me. That was the life I used to live, and Tracey knew it.

She walked behind me in her black freak'um dress and three inch green heels staring at my outfit, probably wondering how I'd gone from riches to rags. She didn't say much more, just shook her head until we got outside the station.

"Where's your car?" I asked, looking around.

"Car? That's funny. Bitch, I barely make enough loot to keep a roof ova' my head. I catch rides with my flava of the month, or rely on pit and pat." She smacked her lips together.

"Who is that?"

"My feet, bitch." She laughed wildly. For some reason, Tracey had that kind of laugh that made other people want to laugh too…Even if you didn't think it was funny. She started walking down Eighth Avenue, but kept talking. "But you can't do that, cuz. We gotta get yo ass some shoes before we do anything else."

I shook my head and followed. We stopped at some

off-brand store to get me some shoes and a jacket, compliments of Tracey. It wasn't what I wanted, but served the purpose.

After that, it took us another thirty minutes to make it to Tracey's apartment on West 127th Street. We didn't talk much on the way there, because she'd been on the phone with someone named Luke the whole time, the guy she called her flava of the month. They talked in codes mostly, with uh hum's and ah umm's. I felt kinda strange, so once we approached her apartment, and she hung up the phone, I asked her if she'd been talking about me. Tracey was my cousin, but I had serious trust issues.

She put her hands on her hips and hesitated before responding. "Damn, girl, you still nosey. But if you must know, yes. I called my friend Luke, 'cause I want him to meet you. He's a playa and knows big people in big places," she smacked, in between words.

I gave her a funny look and crossed my arms. I knew game when it was being dealt. "What is he, a pimp?" I asked. "'Cause I ain't no hoe."

"Shit, you used to be drug dealer, what's the difference," Tracey fired back. At first she had this nonchalant look on her face, until she noticed the sadness in my eyes. "Look, lil' cuz, I'm just an outta shape stripper. I ain't got yo shapely bod, lil' waistline, and big tits," she said with resentment, grabbing one of my nipples at the same time. "I think you got what it takes to make some serious money in this town. I got somethin' better in mind for you."

Damn, those were the exact same words that came from the conductor on the train.

I snatched my breast from Tracey's grip, and followed

her into the apartment. Either my vision was fucked up, or her place was some trash. *A real shit hole*, I thought. I couldn't believe my eyes. As I entered, I stepped on shit like old magazines and dirty panties right at the door. *What the fuck?*

It smelled like a damn dog had pissed all over the place, but there were no pets in sight. I took a few steps forward, trying to find some floor space so I wouldn't fall and bust my ass, when I noticed the unspeakable. This nasty heffa had a dirty sanitary napkin sitting on the edge of the couch. That was it for me. I knew I had to find another place real soon.

Tracey grabbed the pad like it had a right to be there. Then she bent over and picked up a few dirty plates from the floor, as if that little spot cleaning was all she needed to make the place presentable. I thought to myself, you'll need Neicy Nash and the Clean House crew up in this spot. I was so stunned. I found comfort near the wall. I waited for her to say something comforting like, *make yourself at home*.

Instead she said, "Bitch, why you standin' there lookin' retarded? Move that stuff off the couch and sit down. Don't worry, bitch, this the fun house!"

I folded my arms like I always did when in uncomfortable situations, and plopped down in the raggedy cloth chair. My eyes darted to the end of the hall, letting me know Tracey's place was small. There were only two doors to the back of the apartment, which meant a bedroom and a bathroom. *Damn, she really is doing bad.*

Tracey was never the type to hide her feelings, so she started talking about my mother, and the rest of the family who had gotten locked up with us. She wanted to know how it all happened, and why I was the only one who got out. She'd heard the rumors that spread throughout the family, but wanted to hear it straight from me.

I held nothing back. It was actually therapeutic. We talked for hours, while I gave a detailed account of how things got started, who was doing what, and how much money my mother was really making. Before long, Tracey looked at her watch, and jumped up like she was late for work or missing something really important.

She walked over to a tiny hall closet, threw me a worn towel and washcloth, and pointed to the bathroom. "I'll get you a t-shirt and some shorts. Clean yo'self up before Luke gets here."

"I'm not really up to meeting Luke tonight. I need some sleep," I said.

"Look, there's some bologna in the frig. Make yo'self a sandwich and wash yo ass. I'ma be back., I'ma bring Luke," she said, with her hands clutching her flabby hips.

"I don't eat bologna," I said to her backside.

"Well, eat a damn mayo sandwich."

Suddenly, back to back loud knocks banged on Tracey's door. At first I was okay with the loud knocks until I glanced at Tracey. She always played Billy Bad-Ass, but her side-ways funky look made me think she was unsure about who knocked uncontrollably on the other side.

"Who the fuck is it?" she yelled nervously, moving toward her front door. "You ain't let nobody follow you, did you?" she whispered.

I looked crazily wanting to choke her ass. I shook my head back and forth rapidly like a mute. Words weren't important- my life was. If the person on the other side of that door wanted me, I damn sure wasn't gonna let'em hear my voice.

The knocks got louder and Tracey yelled again. "Who is it?"

Still no response.

Tracey backed up slowly as the banging sounds increased. It sounded like somebody was using a pole to punch at the door. "Open the fuckin' door!" a voice yelled.

My body froze, but my eyes remained glued to the door. I hopped up, charged to the left, and did a flip over the back of the couch. Contemplating my next action, my body shook like a vibrating dildo. Whoever was on the other side of the door was serious about getting in. My heart pounded as I thought back to my New Jersey attack. These people really wanted me.

"Tracey, let me the fuck in," another voice shouted.

Next thing I knew, Tracey let a smile slip through her mouth and headed for the door. When she opened it, a young boy looking like he hadn't reached puberty yet walked briskly in the door.

"Winky, I'ma fuck yo ass up?" Tracey belted out.

"Why? You shoulda opened the damn door."

"You out there knocking like the damn police."

"I got it like that…remember, I paid the rent up in this mufucka last month."

"Get yo high- ass outta here."

I stood all the way up figuring things were okay. When I looked Winky in his eye, I could tell he had been smoking. He smelled like a truck load of weed, and walked real jittery all over the apartment.

"Look, I gotta go," Tracey announced. "Whatchu got

for me?"

"A lil' somethin', somethin'."

"Somethin' what? You ain't gettin' no ass."

"Who want your stale- ass pussy? The whole neighborhood had it all ready."

Winky laughed, then asked me if I wanted to smoke a
blunt with him. I just shook my head.

Tracey grabbed Winky's weed smelling ass to the front
door. "I'll be back," she said to me. "Winky take yo simple ass home," she ended.

The front door slammed hard when they left. Tracey
never even turned back to look me in my face. *Some hos-
pitality*, I thought, bringing all these simple ass niggas in
her house. *And Luke, he can forget about me.*

I felt like I was being pimped, but knew I wasn't
gonna work the streets or live in a run down spot like
Tracey's. I was determined to make a way for myself,
even if I had to resort to getting in touch with Agent
Barnes. Without a dime to my name, I showered, fixed
my hair, and made room to lie on the wobbly cloth couch,
waiting for Tracey to come back.

By the time she came in, I had one eye open, praying
it wasn't another ambush. My eyes opened wide when a
fairly thin guy stumbled past me. His face couldn't be
made in the darkness, but the smell of Hennessey reeking
from his pores filled the air. Between knocking down pic-
tures and bumping into the furniture, Tracey guided his
way, cursing him out in the process. I expected her to
come back out and introduce us after he made it to the
room. Instead, twenty minutes later, she peeped out from
her door in a freaky laced outfit, and turned off the hall
light. The moment her door closed, I shut my look-out

eye, and drifted into a light sleep.

Chapter Five

The next morning, a crunching sound woke me up early. A shabbily dressed guy, who resembled Terrance Howard from the movie *Hustle and Flow* stared me in the face. He sat in an oversized bean bag, peeling an apple with a sharp looking knife. My eyes damn near busted through my head.

"This Luke," Tracey said, walking up behind him. "Luke, this my cuz, Candice. Didn't I tell you she was a dime piece, real fineeeeeeeee," she bragged.

I looked at Tracey like I wanted to kill her, not just because she had a wannabe hustler in front of me, but also because I hated the way she dragged her words sometimes, and always ended with a smack.

Luke never took his eyes off of me. He just kept mumbling, "Umph...umph...umph...oh, yeah, we gotta winner."

I stretched, and wiped the crust from my eyes. I'd obviously slept all night, and good too. My nervousness slowly went away, but his demeanor still made me feel a little uncomfortable. I wasn't sure why, 'cause he wasn't the type of guy I would normally be fearful of. As a matter of fact, his Louisiana twang didn't make me think he was harmful at all.

"She might work," he told Tracey.

"Might? Hell, my cuz is pretty as shit," she responded.

"I heard you were a snitch," Luke blurted out, while taking another bite of his apple.

I sat up straight, and gave Tracey the evil eye. My arms were folded across one another and clenched tightly.

"Nah..uhhhhh," Tracey said, in my defense. She pushed his shoulder. "I told you she got locked up for nothin', right along with my aunt, uncles, two cousins, and her man. It wasn't her fault. They had the drug ring goin'. She just lived wit'em and got caught up."

"Yeah, well, where I'm from, that's called snitchin', if they all still in and you out." He cut another slice of his apple, gobbled it down, and stared right back into my face. "The people I'm tryin' to hook her up wit', they lookin' for loyal broads. Broads who ain't bringin' no trouble, and no police either." Luke looked at me as if to ask, if I was bringing trouble.

"Look, I'm not on trial! And I didn't ask you to come here!" I shouted. I looked at Tracey for some help. She looked back at Luke, giving him the eye to stop.

"Bet…your loss. Tracey told me you needed a good job one better than hers. She said you had the look." He got up, threw his tye-dyed hoodie on over his wife-beater, and walked toward the kitchen. He looked back for another quick look at me. "You do got the look though," he added. "You could make a lot of cash, and live good too. You get to live at the spot while on payroll. I'm talkin' 'bout a mini-mansion in a suburban neighborhood and shit."

I turned and looked at Luke with a lil' interest. I liked

the sound of that, 'cause I definitely didn't want to stay at
Tracey's spot too long. It was loud, and in the heart of
everything. "What I gotta do?" I asked, with an attitude.
"Long as it ain't no prostitute shit."

"Nah...it's like an escort service. You gotta be the dates
of high profile people; you know senators, politicians,
musicians and shit." Luke moved closer to me, and
rubbed his thumb from the top of my face down to the
side of my cheek. "Your smooth cocoa skin and long hair
will have 'em goin' crazy. Not to mention that bad ass
body you got. It's my manz spot. He'll look out for you.
Just make you some money and roll," he suggested.

Luke had a point. It couldn't have been too much
worse than when I worked for my mother. I thought back
to how Big V ran her business. It was a tight ship; but it
was all about family. Between me, my uncles Ray and
Cedric, and my man Rich, we sold most of the coke in the
Brooklyn and Queens area. Big V never touched any
product. She met the connec', and then her brother,
Kenny, was responsible for cooking up all the coke and
distributing it in the streets. That's where I came in.

I remember wearing many hats. Some days, I'd have
to meet drug dealers, sell them the shit, and collect the
money. Other times, I'd have to take a drive with the
money to pay off what we'd been fronted. So many times,
I thought about driving off with thousands of Big V's
money, never to show my face again.

One time, I even drove two kilo's of raw coke to Big
V's favorite client. It was the night I was supposed to go
out with Rich on Valentine's Day. She screamed like
crazy, telling me to get my fuckin' ass in that car and
drive that shit to meet her boy, some Jamaican dude. I

remember feeling like a whipped puppy, 'cause there was no talking back to Big V. Especially when she said that's what the hell she bought me my convertible CLK for... *to drive her shit around.*

Back then there were no tears, just unhappiness. On the outside, I was getting money, and had the best looking guy in town. But nobody understood that I was locked up already, mentally that is.

"You a' ight?" Luke interrupted. "No time for day dreamin' and shit. Get up, get ready, and slap on some good smells."

"I didn't say I was going!"

"What? You gon' stay here with Tracey? C'mon, man, you know better."

I frowned, knowing he was right. I just didn't want to be led by a hoodlum, who couldn't even keep his pants up on his waist. "Okay…I'll go," I finally agreed. "But not for long. Just until I make enough money to move away and be on my own."

"Bet. I just gotta spring for an outfit before you start. You make a nigga look bad, goin' over there lookin' broke down."

I stretched my neck, wanting to ask him if he'd looked in the mirror lately. It looked like he had slapped a bunch of gel in his two-inch strands dressed like a starved thug.

"Let's move it then," Luke ordered, with an instant grin. He moved his hands back and forth, motioning me to move faster. I took my time getting dressed, and questioned Tracey like crazy about her strange flavor of the month.

Before long, we were on 125th Street, and had hit up one of Luke's thieving friends for a new outfit just for me. He had all kinds of stuff, ranging from Baby Phat to Apple Bottoms, to no name sweatsuits and athletic gear. I wanted more, but Luke said he was doing me a favor just to get me in the door. He said first impressions were long lasting. I laughed inside, wondering what catalog Tracey had gotten this clown from.

We made several stops in the city before heading out to meet Luke's connection with the job opening. The ride to Long Island gave me time to really think. In between Luke's ranting and raving about his friend Duece, I mapped out my plan. I'd decided that I would only stay at Duece's house for a few months, just enough time to make some money and move to L.A., or maybe even Vegas, just somewhere far away. Until then, maybe this new spot would be incognito.

From what Luke said, it didn't seem like nobody from the streets would be coming anywhere near his place. Luke said Duece was from the streets, and had a notorious rep from back in the day, but was now all about business. He only rubbed shoulders with the elite, and kept the low lives far away from his establishment.

Luke slammed on breaks, taking me away from my thoughts. He backed the white Impala up quickly, making sure his tires screeched in the process. Through the black rod iron gates, what looked to me like a mini-mansion, sat nestled back behind the gigantic flower beds.

"What's that address?" Luke asked, leaning in front of Tracey. "I can't see shit."

"Hell if I know. If you can't see it, why you think I can," she smacked. "And get your Jheri curl out my face," she joked.

"Right there," he pointed. "The address is on the

columns. That's it," he added, in a more serious tone.

Luke whipped the car around and pulled up to the gate. I thought we were gonna have to push a button on the intercom and give names along with I.D. Strangely, the gate opened as we pulled onto the cobblestone driveway. The house sat like a mansion up on top of the hill. The only way up to the front door was the long expensive looking stairwell, which led to the stylish landing.

"See, didn't I tell you your boy was gonna hook shit up," Luke boasted, shaking his head up and down. His smile grew wider the closer we got to the front of the house. He leaned over and kissed Tracey. "You wanna cut, don't you?"

Tracey rolled her eyes and didn't even respond. I wasn't sure if he was joking or not, but focused my attention to the opening French doors above the stoned staircase. When the car stopped, we hopped out and followed closely behind Luke. He walked like he'd done this before, and made it clear that he admired Deuce's style.

I walked slowly up the stairs, only to see a huge man emerge and shake Luke's hand out on the landing. "Long time no see," the man said to Luke. "And this pretty lady is?" he asked, referring to Tracey. His cologne was loud, but smelled real good and expensive. He placed an arm on Tracey's shoulder, like he felt sorry for her. It was almost as if he knew she wasn't the one coming to work for him.

Luke jumped over near Tracey quickly and began pulling me closer. "This my girl, Tracey, and this here is her cousin, Candice." He grinned like he'd won a prize and was sharing it with his boy.

I was starting to think Luke was going to benefit

somehow for referring me, 'cause he was way too happy about seeing me at the house with his friend.

"How are you, Candice?" Duece asked suspiciously.

"Fine," I answered, in a low voice. I avoided meeting his eyes, but could feel his stare. I pulled up the sleeves on the tight chocolate colored velour sweatsuit, and prayed he'd turn his eyes elsewhere. Suddenly, I realized they were all looking at me, even Tracey.

"Did I do something wrong, Duece?" I asked.

He let out a sarcastic laugh. "Duece? My name is Daddy," he responded, in a cockier tone.

"Oh, Luke said your name was Duece."

He didn't respond with words, he just threw Luke a frown.

"Nahhhhhh, don't get me late with this big muthafuc-ka. I call'em Duece, cause I don't feel right calling a big greasy nigga, Daddy," Luke explained.

We all laughed, which broke the ice. I crossed my arms and tried to loosen up a bit, while Daddy continued to look at me through the corner of his eyes. His golden skin tone glistened in the sun, which made me squint just a little. He was a large man, pushing 320 pounds. Far from solid, I noticed he wore his clothes well. He appeared to be in his late forties, and immediately remind-ed me of an older Suge Knight-thick beard and all.

"Man, I told her you'on take no shit," Luke bragged.

Daddy just nodded, keeping his eyes on me.

"So, we in?" Luke questioned, like a fidgety junkie.

"We?" Daddy asked sarcastically. He turned around and opened the front door to the house slightly. When he called out to someone, I instantly got nervous. *What if Big V is inside and this is all a trick?*

Daddy's House

"She'll do," Daddy spoke with confidence. "Why don't you two leave us be. Let Miss Candice here get settled in," he ordered, without even raising his voice. "I've gotta run, but the woman who handles things around here is on her way down to meet her now." Daddy extended his hand toward me with another scrutinizing look. "We'll meet again soon." He appeared to be still a little unsure about me, but the slight opening of the door distracted him.

A woman dressed in navy blue business attire appeared at the front door with a clipboard in hand. Her expression was far from warm when Daddy introduced us.

"Dottie, Candice will be working here starting today. Get her settled. I'll catcha later."

"Hmm..umm," she uttered, with a smirk.

Daddy turned to leave off the landing, headed down the steps. Luke quickly followed behind. Tracey, on the other hand, was on my heels ready to enter the house with me.

"Oh, I'll take it from here," Dottie firmly stated, letting Tracey know she wasn't welcomed.

I turned to let Tracey know it was okay, when I saw the buck expression on her face. "Just who the hell do you think you are?" she belted. "With that short, wack-ass hair-do." She gritted her teeth, rolled her eyes, and carried on like she wanted me to be fired before I was officially hired. I got sidetracked when I saw Daddy over Tracey's shoulder hand Luke some money. I wasn't sure if it was a loan, or a finder's fee.

"It's okay, Tracey. Really...I'll be okay. I'll call you," I ended.

"Shiiid…don't lemme have to fuck nobody up out this mufucka!"

While Tracey was ranting and raving, Dottie pulled me completely inside and was shutting the door in her face. Suddenly, Tracey stuck her business card through the tiny slit.

"Call me on my cell phone if you need me!" she yelled, through the door crack. "I know you don't have the number." Then, just that quick, a thumping sound ended our view of one another.

I stood in the foyer with Dottie alone, looking like an alien in new territory. I figured playing the shy role would convince her to cut me some slack and be more welcoming. Wrong. She looked downward, like I was beat up in the face and unbearable to look at. Not even worthy. I reacted by looking toward the sparkling chandelier above my head. I told myself this would be my last humiliation in life.

"Follow me," she ordered.

"Okay," I responded, noticing her huge round key ring that resembled a miniature hoola hoop. It reminded me of the one Bookman carried on *Good Times*. But Ms. Dottie was far from a jokester like him. She was tough, didn't even crack a damn smile.

I held Tracey's card close to my chest. She was my last hope. That was when I knew things had gone sour for me. Although I would temporarily reside in the fabulous house, which was decorated like something on MTV Cribs, I still felt homeless.

As I walked quickly behind Ms. Dottie, trying to keep up, a nicely decorated office to my left caught my attention. A young white chick, dressed in a stretchy rayon booty length dress, sat at a computer, with her legs spread wide open, and raised up on the desk. She laughed and played with her hair, like she was talking to someone special. Even Ms. Dottie looked at her strangely, but kept her focus on me.

"I just realized you didn't bring your bags," she said, stopping abruptly.

"I don't have any."

"Oh…that's a first," she responded. "Moving right along," she smirked, and started walking again.

The house was plush, and the hardwood floors looked like they'd been freshly waxed. Ms. Dottie led me to a set of double doors and opened them wide. "Candice, this is what we call the showroom. This room is where you'll be showing the guys what you got, like these ladies here," she said, pointing her index finger.

I realized at that moment what I'd gotten myself into. Turning three shades of purple, I held the lower part of my stomach. Roughly, six women were laid around the large room in nasty, freaky attire. Satin, lace, chenille, you name it, it was on their bodies. I stood there for a moment, not even realizing that Ms. Dottie was introducing me. My focus was on the Asian woman spread out on the zebra print rug with a dildo pressed against the side of her face. I coughed out loud like I was having some type of asthma attack. Inside, my breakdown was coming. This was it. I couldn't take anymore.

In between my coughs, I asked, "Which way to the bathroom?"

Ms. Dottie just pointed, and followed behind me like a small toddler.

I could hear the chuckles from behind, just as my

stomach knotted up inside. *Why didn't Tracey tell me*, I wondered. *Does she know the real deal? This shit is far beyond dates.* "Escort my ass!" I blurted out.

I ran inside the bathroom, slammed the door, and lifted the toilet seat so hard it almost came off the hinges. I felt so sick; a deep down sickness, deep in the pit of my stomach. I felt guilty as I threw up all over the gold plated accessories. With vomit splattered all over the toilet, I figured this was the end. *Gross*, I thought. *No, Just plain nasty!*

"Come out of there," I heard a voice say. "This is a community bathroom!"

Damn, I couldn't even be sick in peace. Besides, I needed time to think. Loud knocks like the police banged on the door repeatedly. I needed to think about whether I'd make a run for it or just walk out and tell Ms. Dottie that there was a miscommunication. They didn't tell me I'd be a slut.

"What's going on in there?" Ms. Dottie yelled.

"I'm okay," I mumbled. "Be out in a sec."

I used what was left of the toilet tissue roll to wipe the remaining gook from my mouth. I looked in the mirror as the knocking got louder. "Come out of there!" Ms. Dottie shouted.

I snatched the door open, and breathed a heavy sigh. Still flush in the face, I asked if I could see where I'd be sleeping. I really didn't want to do it, but I'd made my mind up. It was my final answer. I was staying. I would stay long enough to get myself on my feet. Then I'd be out. Where else would I go? Back to Tracey's dump with Luke, waiting for his next scheme?

I wiped my wet hands on my sweatsuit, and tried to

look like I had some dignity left as Ms. Dottie told me to follow her upstairs. The moment I got to the first step, a beautiful woman, dark like milk chocolate, strutted her way down the steps. The way she walked commanded attention. I wasn't gay, but I knew an attractive woman when I saw one. I'd already given her a ten, until she bumped me purposely and her bad boob job was exposed.

"Looks like Daddy hired a pregnant trick this time," she joked, followed by a nasty stare.

I instantly looked down at my wash board stomach, to see if the sweatsuit was making me look pudgy. I'd always prided myself on my Janet Jackson abs.

"I mean…she must be pregnant, throwing up and shit."

"Mind your business, Cat!" Ms. Dottie yelled. You know we don't allow that type of shit in Daddy's House. We're here to make money. That's it."

"Of course I know that," she spat. "I make the most money, don't I?"

She looked at me one last time, like the statement was really meant for me to know. I didn't know whether I should've said something to prove I wasn't a punk, or just tripped the tall bitch. Instead, Ms. Dottie handled it, probably because she thought I was weak.

"Cat, take your jealous-ass on. Every time we get a little competition in here, you wanna run them away. Honey, follow me to your room." She brought her focus back to me. "Moving right along," she mumbled softly, like she was reminding herself to get focused again.

I followed, noticing how thick Ms. Dottie's hair appeared to be. Her short pen curls were matted to her head, and looked like she'd used a jar of beeswax that morning. When we made it to the top of the staircase, I turned to see Cat still at the bottom of the stairs, with her arms folded and her mouth twitched like she had a beef to settle. *Damn, will my life ever have any peace? I even gotta watch my back in a hoe house.*

Chapter Six

The next day I got up early with a master plan. Four months was gonna seem like a lifetime, but depending on how much paper I could make per month, that's how long I was willing to stick it out. I rushed into the small bathroom inside my bedroom and took a quick shower. I wanted to get downstairs to that computer I'd seen yesterday before the other girls got up. I needed to search the internet for my mother. Tracey told me to go to some fed's website and type in her name, to see if she was still locked up. She was a dangerous woman, and I didn't trust her. I couldn't help but wonder if she had planned the ambush on me, and who was helping her. *Damn, I hope Rich is not involved.*

Surprisingly, when I stepped out of the shower, a brand new red silk robe was laid neatly on the bed, with matching thongs. I hadn't heard anyone come in, so I tip-toed, with my towel wrapped tightly, closer to the door. Still, no sign of anyone. I figured it must've been Ms. Dottie, 'cause she was the only one with keys to every-body's room.

I quickly moistened my body with a bottle of lotion that was on the nightstand. I guess it was in place for whoever stayed in the room. Smelling like a sweet orange, I dressed in my new red panties and the same sweatsuit from the day before, realizing I didn't have any other clothes to wear downstairs.

"I sure as hell ain't gonna wear that robe downstairs," I said to myself.

Anxiously I headed to the door, only to be met by Ms. Dottie and her infamous clipboard and oversized key ring. She rushed inside my room, and gave me a serious inspection. Dressed for a power meeting, she had on a pin stripped shirt, some fancy wide legged pants, and expensive Ferragamo shoes.

"Just where do you think you're going in that outfit?" she asked, her hand moving back and forth swiftly. "Take it all off," she instructed, not even giving me a chance to respond. "You can't walk around like that anymore. I have some things for you."

She opened the bedroom door and reached for something outside. A big white bag filled with clothes was pulled inside; while she tossed a black low cut shirt my way and some matching Capri pants. My jaw hung low as I watched her pull out sets of provocative, sluttish outfits from the bag. I just stood there, wondering when the bottom was near. Unfortunately for me, none of it was my style of clothing.

"Take it all off now," she said again in a louder voice, and headed toward the small closet off to the side. She took a moment, rummaging through the different keys, in search of the right one. "Finally," she said, with a heavy sigh.

"Who's clothes are these?" I asked with a frown.

She ignored the shit outta me. When Ms. Dottie unlocked the door, I thought I was in the Macy's shoe department. Lines of shoes, ranging in all sizes, stared me in the face. "And wear these today for weekly meeting."

The black three-inch stilletto's she handed me was perfect for hitting the streets in search of a buck. I gritted my teeth and hesitantly slid them on. I stood in the middle of the floor with underwear, a push up bra that accented my young, perky breasts, and stilettos to add that extra height, listening to instruction after instruction.

"Now, get dressed, someone is coming to your room in a few minutes."

I formed a blank expression on my face. Everything was happening so fast, I didn't think to ask who. I just listened.

"The meeting is in the showroom and starts at noon, *sharp*. That's not nigga noon. It's 12:00 p.m., one minute after 11:59 a.m. You understand?" Ms. Dottie paced the floor like a militant soldier. "You looking at me like you're a little slow." She waited for a response, but I didn't give one.

"You have a hair appointment with Claude, the house hairstylist at one o'clock today, and a nail appointment at two. Remember, keep yourself looking good at all times…you never know when *Big Money* will show up. Always be prepared for an opportunity," she added. "Oh…and most importantly, when you get downstairs today, leave your snobbish attitude right here."

"Me?" I pointed at myself in shock.

"Moving right along."

I was starting to realize that's what she said when she was done with the conversation. "No problem," I responded. "I may need some help with the computer when I get downstairs. Is there a password?"

"Make friends. Ask one of the girls," she smirked. "I'm not a computer tech, but they will determine whether you make it around here or not."

Damn, I thought. *She's rougher than I expected.* My plan was to be cordial, but new friends I didn't need. I'd already decided that I was gonna be sociable and make the best of my situation. I'd even practiced my fake smile in the mirror when I first got up.

"That's it," Ms. Dottie said, placing a big check on the paper in front of her. "Now…" A double knock at the door interrupted her words. "I guess he's here." She looked at me kinda funny. "No need to get dressed now. On the bed and spread 'em." She grinned widely.

No…you…can't be serious? I thought. Not this soon. What if this guy asked for something I wasn't willing to do? Would I be out on the streets my first full day here?

The door swung open and a tall, attractive, slender man in his late fifties walked inside. His salt and pepper beard stood out. *Distinguished*, I thought. Reminded me of one of my uncles. He pulled his leather briefcase that was on wheels, as he walked into the room, and adjusted the suit jacket hanging over his shoulder. Although he seemed a bit arrogant, he smiled a pleasant smile, like we'd met each other before. When he extended his hand, I didn't even shake it. Nervously, I wondered what I'd have to do. Tracey had told me I'd have to entertain a few politicians…he surely looked like one.

"Hello, I'm Doctor Charles," he said. "From the look on your face, I guess Ms. Dottie didn't tell you I was coming today."

I loosened up a bit, and was finally able to speak. "No…no, she didn't," I replied, looking Ms. Dottie in her face.

"Be nice," she instructed, pushing Doctor Charles' small stool inside the door. "See you at the meeting," she added, shutting the door on her way out.

Alone with Doctor Charles, I felt bare, even though I was half-naked anyway.

I was confused. Not sure whether he had showed up for a good time or to offer his services, I asked, "What's this all about? I mean, that throw up thing last night was just 'cause I couldn't stop coughing."

"Oh really?" He laughed.

"Yeah, really."

"Well, Candice, what if I told you I didn't know anything about you throwing up?" he asked, bending down to take several instruments from his bag.

I looked at him strangely, as he placed the items on a white towel that covered the small coffee table. When he pulled out what looked like an instrument, probably used to give an abortion, I panicked.

"Well, what are you here for? And are all of those for me?" I pointed.

"I have to give you an exam to see if you're clean. You know Daddy's clients spend a great deal of money in here, so it's my job to make sure you don't harm them. Have you been naughty?" He laughed, slipping his gloves on. "Tell me now, before we get started."

"Hell yeah I'm clean. What you tryna say?"

He laughed again. "That's what they all say. Trust me, I'll be back next week to help you clear up your yeast infection or some nasty drip."

I wanted to slap the shit outta him, but it wasn't worth it. He wasn't paying me no mind anyway. If I didn't know better, I'd think I was really in a doctor's office, by the number of medical items he'd pulled out his bag. He stood like he was ready to perform surgery, as he pulled out several clear 2x2 plastic containers. "Now take your underwear off and lay back," he instructed.

"Where?" I asked, looking around the room.

"Where else…on the bed silly."

"Waittttttt," I stuttered. "Are you a real doctor? Like you went to school and all that?" I asked, backing up toward the bed.

"Yes, and all that," he responded sarcastically. "Now, let's get started. I get paid by the hour. You definitely don't want to get on Daddy's bad side already, newbie." He grinned, as I took my thongs off and laid flat on the bed.

"A little bit wider." He smiled and moved toward the end of the bed, pulling the stool over at the same time. Instantly, my nose was flooded with the smell of vinegar and other sanitizing smells.

I spread my legs a lil' more, uneasy about his touch. His hands were unbelievably warm. They moved about my body seductively, from the top of my thighs to the bottom of my ass. When he whisked past my pubic hairs, like he was looking for something, I almost lost it. I'd never had an exam where the doctor rubbed and prodded as much as this clown did. He asked me a few lame questions, like when was my last period, and how many sex partners I'd had in the last five years. When I told him two…he almost fell off the stool.

"No…seriously?" he asked.

"I am serious," I replied, as my eyes rolled toward the ceiling. Surely I lied with a straight face.

BY AZAREL

Before I knew it, he'd pulled out the speculum, and
proceeded to give me a pap smear. I wanted to yell out so
someone could be in the room with me, but I'd already
performed the night before. So I laid back and prayed Ms.
Dottie would come back in. Soon, Doctor Charles was
done with phase one. He stood up like he'd just got a nut.
His constant grinning made me sick. The way he squirted
the gel on his finger made me think he was really insane.

"Now, this may feel a little cold," he said. "So just
relax."

I squirmed and tightened my ass, preparing for his fingers. He placed one of his hands on my stomach, trying to
relax my body, and then sneakily moved toward my
breast. The moment he inserted his fingers, his eyebrows
creased, showing his pleasure. He moved and fingered me
like he was my man, while cupping my breast with his
other hand. At first my muscles resisted, holding out for a
few seconds, waiting for him to be done. Then, when I
noticed his fingers were planted firmly in place, I loosened up, wondering what was next.

To my surprise, he started to massage the inside of my
walls. The sane part of me told me to jump up and kick
Doctor Charles in his damn face. But the selfish part of
me enjoyed what I thought was happening. His fingers
continued to grind and dance all in my pussy until his
glove became drenched. I was so overdue, considering I
hadn't been wet in six months. Squeaking noises erupted,
and became quicker and louder by the minute. Even
worse, his hardness grazing against my ass cheeks signaled more trouble. Before I knew it, I was in ecstasy. I
kept looking back and forth toward the door, wondering if
Ms. Dottie was gonna come in, or if this was all a test.

63

Then I snapped.

Our eyes met and he looked away, like he couldn't bear to look me in the face. I reached for the upper part of his arm, which resisted at first, but then roughly pushed him away. My wetness continued to drip, as he backed up, trying to map out his next move.

Instantly he packed up, throwing his things like a wild man into his bag. He slammed one of the plastic containers on the dresser with harsh instructions, "Piss in the cup and leave it on the dresser. Ms. Dottie will take care of it for me."

I sat up on the bed and threw the sheet across my body like I'd just been raped. "I hope you enjoyed yourself," I snapped.

"Sure did," he shot back.

My eyes bulged out of my head. I couldn't believe he was openly admitting to being a pervert. "We'll see how long you continue to practice after I report your ass!" I screamed, like I meant business.

He chuckled. "Go ahead. I'm sure they'll believe a hooker."

Damn, is that what I am? I felt worthless. I didn't even get paid.

"Go 'head. Tell who the hell you want. They won't believe you. You're a high paid trick. You'll just be named a troublemaker." He let out a wild laugh, and walked toward the door. "You could've stopped me," he ended, and shut the door.

I stood up, still wet and numb. I didn't know how to feel or what to say. A part of me wanted to run and scrub my skin while another part said, *just get used to it, you've been through worse.*

Chapter Seven

An hour later, I was downstairs sitting on the sofa, waiting for our meeting to start. I scanned the room out the corner of my eye, as each girl walked in one by one and took their spot on the carpet, or plopped down wherever they were most comfortable. I could tell the meeting would be informal by the way everyone strutted in nonchalantly. Most of the girls were standoffish except a brown-skinned girl, who was overly friendly. She was originally from the south and spoke with a twang.

"Hi I'm Cinnamon, and you must be the new girl," she announced, with a warm welcome. She sat her barely one hundred pound body on the edge of the couch next to me, not even interested in a real seat.

I smiled back, hoping that I'd made at least one friend, because at that moment, Cat walked in, towering over me and all the girls, and sat directly next to me. She shot me the hardest look possible. *Of all places to sit, why near me?* Her height intimidated me a bit, only because she was tall like my mother, but I turned my head and watched the other girls enter the room.

By the time Ms. Dottie cleared her throat, I had counted about eight girls in all. We came in all sizes, and apparently many different attitudes. The same Asian chick, who was laying on the floor with the dildo the day before, abruptly walked in and sashayed across the floor, headed to the far corner of the room. We all looked at her strangely as she kneeled, not wanting to sit or stand. She started doing squats with a disgruntled look on her face. She stared directly at Ms. Dottie, like she had a problem with her, but paused every so often and performed another squat.

"Listen up, Kitty Cats," Ms. Dottie began, "I have a few things on the agenda."

I watched as two Hispanic looking girls, who sat side by side, make jokes under their breath. They never looked my way, but I watched them closely. Hell, I was watching everybody.

"Some things are getting out of hand around here," Ms. Dottie uttered. "And it needs to stop now. Some people are abusing their time in the gym." She paused and walked around the room. "You know who you are."

"Be woman and just say," the Asian chick blurted out, and stood to her feet. "You mad 'cause I look good…tasty… so…lickable," she teased, turning in a circle and making her ass jiggle from the back.

At that moment I noticed the nose ring that adorned her face. She was a strange looking woman, sorta manly, yet sexy in her own way. The more she moved, the more I noticed her shape. She was obviously serious about working out. Her stomach was flat as mine, and perfect for her body piercings.

"Sit your nasty-ass down, Sushi," Ms. Dottie spoke firmly. "Rules are rules. You get one hour per day to keep yourself looking good. Use it or lose it. Otherwise, keep your ass outta the gym. It's too small for more than three people at a time. Besides, it's not your house…it's Daddy's. And I run the show around this place."

"Me house too!" Sushi shouted, pointing her finger down south. "Daddy tell me that."

"Shut the fuck up, Chica!" one of the Hispanic girls yelled. At that moment, it dawned on me that they were twins.

"No…no…you shut up, School Teacher!" she shouted, in her thick Asian accent. "Can you see me through glasses?" The entire room burst into laughter.

Even though I wasn't sure if I got the joke, I assumed Sushi called one the Hispanic chicks School Teacher because of her red round-shaped eyeglasses. Besides, the granny smith apple that she was eating didn't help her image either.

"Sushi, this is my final warning!" Ms. Dottie shouted, in a firmer tone.

Sushi clearly wasn't a real threat to anyone. She was just upset. Eventually, she sat down, but not before passing evil stares around the room. Strangely, she omitted me and two other black girls, who only paid Ms. Dottie attention. They seemed to be serious about their business and not interested in all the drama.

"That goes for you too, School Teacher," Ms Dottie added. "Oh, while I'm on you, we had a complaint last week about you not wanting to take off your glasses while you were with a client. Now, Daddy has told you about that before, so if you refuse to get contacts, then you're gonna find yourself out of here."

School Teacher bit into her apple and shook her head. "I'm gonna go get the contacts, I promise."

"You better. I don't know what you need to see anyway. Just lay on your back and make that money," Ms. Dottie continued. "Okay my next point...days off! This is the situation. You need to be bleeding from the mouth or have HIV to take a day off other than what you're assigned. We got bills to pay, so stop pretending to have issues when you need to be on your back! By the way, Candice, you're new, so you got Mondays off." She looked at me, making sure I understood.

I nodded.

"Yeah, bitch...you at the bottom of the barrel," Cat spat.

She looked at me and rolled her eyes. I'd never done anything to this woman, yet she was treating me like her worst enemy.

"She not like, 'cause you pretty," Sushi remarked.

"Shut up, you non-talking, bitch!" Cat yelled.

"That's enough," Ms. Dottie interrupted, giving Cat another stare. "Moving right along." Her hardened look said it better be over.

Cat folded her arms and crossed her legs as the meeting continued. I slid Tracey's crumbled up business card out of my pocket, and held it tightly in the palm of my hand. I needed a pep talk to make it through the day.

Besides, I needed to ask her why the fuck would she set me up like this? I had managed to block out everything Ms. Dottie was saying, until she covered the time allowed to wash clothes, phone and computer time. Everything was done on a schedule, and it was obvious she ran a tight ship. Soon, we were all graced with a surprise. Daddy walked in wearing a tailored black suit, and a pair of expensive looking black loafers with huge silver

G's embedded on the front. Gucci of course. I had good taste in mens' shoes, after all I used to shop for my *ex-love* all the time.

Once Daddy walked in, the mood changed. All the girls sat up nice and tall, like the principal was in the building. At first he just nodded, continuously looking all around the room at each of us carefully. "Did everyone meet Candice?" he asked, standing with his hands in his pockets.

"Me did," Sushi announced, with a grin.

"What up, Candice? Hello, Candice," they all started to say. Even Cat said hello, in a somber tone under her breath.

"Treat her good," he instructed. "She's sexy and gon be a money maker around here. New blood is always good," he promoted. "It's what we need. You feel me?"

"Sure do, Daddy," one of the younger white girls responded. They all started giving their fake responses one after another. He seemed to put fear into the room, and everyone had quickly changed their fucked up behavior.

"By the way…Candice, you're now Candy."

I pointed to myself, just to be sure he meant me. A lump formed in my throat when he looked back at me.

"Yes, you! Every girl in the house has a nickname. Yours is Candy. It's final," he said, with authority. "I think it fits you."

I just smiled, considering his expression showed that I didn't have a choice. Luckily, Ms. Dottie stepped in front of him, giving me time to pick my jaw up off the floor. I was still in shock.

"I've got money," Daddy said, waving some white

envelopes in the air. "Your pay is gooooooooooood this week. Remember, the more money the house makes, the more money you make. Now, before I give these out, I wanna remind you about tomorrow night. It's a big night. I want everybody up in here to look like Rock stars. You feel me?"

We all nodded.

"The Music Expo is in town tomorrow night, and of course, who did they choose to host the brothas in the rap and music game?"

"You Daddy," they all chimed. I got in on the last part. I knew I had to learn fast.

"Yeah, you Daddy," I said softly. He obviously liked his ego stroked.

"These high rollas is ready to spend money. I told'em we got the best pussy in town. Show time is at midnight. So be ready. Don't let me down, or there's a price to pay. You remember what happened to Lisa, don't you?"

Nobody said a word. You could've heard a feather drop, which kinda freaked me out. He stood in the middle of the floor, shaking his head up and down, and looking at each of us for moments at a time. Damn, the whole situation gave me the creeps. *Who is Lisa, and where the hell is she now?*

Daddy handed the envelopes off to Ms. Dottie, and all the girls jumped up, crowding around her, signaling that the meeting was over. Daddy walked over to me and stared before cupping my breasts. "These babies are gonna make me a lot of money," he said, with a huge grin. "Consider yourself my new asset."

His asset. Damn, I was flattered, but a little concerned at the same time.

Cat watched nearby, and her face wrinkled like unfolded laundry. Strangely, Ms. Dottie was disturbed by Daddy's extra attention toward me too. She didn't have to say anything, I just knew the look. When School Teacher walked over to talk to Daddy, it was my chance to leave. I hopped up and made a b-line toward the door. I figured it would be a good time to get on the computer while everyone was getting their loot.

I hurried down the hall and into the office where the computer was. *Damn, the antique desk must've cost a fortune,* I thought when I entered. The room was small and cozy, and didn't contain much more than a phone, a high-back leather chair, and a nice sized Dell computer. I looked at the phone and thought about calling Tracey first, but then I hit the button on the computer and the screen popped on. Just my luck, I hadn't even gotten my passcode yet, but I was on.

Instantly, I started typing www.hmprisonservice.gov. The website popped up, and I typed in my mother's name. I leaned back in the chair and waited with anticipation. When her picture popped up, it scared me half to death. The closeness of the photo revealed her high cheek bones and flawless dark brown skin. Her hair was swooped up in a ponytail, and had obviously not been done. Still in all, she was beautiful. I leaned closer into the computer screen just staring. The bad memories made me shiver.

I thought about the time when she got into a fight with some loud mouth chick at a Frankie Beverly and Maze show. We looked real good in three-inch heels, bomb dresses, and the best purses money could buy. My mother looked so good nobody knew how hood she really was. Before security made it to her side to break up the fight, she'd gutted the girl like a fish, and had passed her knife off to someone who wasn't even with us.

I suddenly snapped out of it and took a deep breath. I looked back at the screen and read the red writing under release date. I panicked.

RELEASED it read in big bold letters. I panted like a forty-two week old pregnant woman in labor. I took quick short breaths in sets of threes, like I was preparing to give birth. I swirled around in my chair, unsure about what to do next. My heart sunk into the depths of my stomach. I leaned down to the floor then back up again. Without prompting, one hand reached for the phone, and the other for Tracey's business card all at the same time. My fingers punched the number keys hard and quick. By the third ring, I felt like I'd already died. When she answered, I just started jumbling all my words.

"Tracey, she's out," I whispered. "Whaaa…t should I…"

"What the fuck are you talkin' about Candice?" Tracey questioned.

"My mother. I went on the site."

"Bitch, you playin'?"

"No… no…listen to…" I stopped mid-sentence. Ms. Dottie was staring over my shoulder like I was a teenager and she was my momma. "Ah huh," I said into the receiver. "Oh, no," I continued, making up conversation along the way. Tracey wasn't saying shit. I started pretending like I was answering questions from someone, like it was a business call. I hadn't received my phone time yet, but from the look on Ms. Dotties's face, I wasn't supposed to be on the phone.

Before I knew it she scribbled a few words down on

her clipboard and ripped the pink sheet off her pad and handed it to me. It was a fine. Circled with a black marker, $100.00 was written in the fine section. This broad had given me a fuckin' fine for being on the phone. My lips puckered, but I didn't say anything, 'cause Daddy walked up behind her, showing his disapproval.

"Don't you think a fine is unnecessary this early in the game? Baby girl just got here."

I didn't hear what Ms. Dottie said, because Tracey was yelling into the receiver. "What the fuck is goin' on over dat mufucka? Why you actin' like you can't have a normal conversation? What kinda shit is that? You might need to leave…now."

Daddy escorted Ms. Dottie away from the door, and surprisingly glanced at the screen. He frowned, and just walked away. If he thought anything, he was too cool to show it. I tried to keep my face looking as normal as possible, and turned my attention back to Tracey, while hitting the x on the screen at the same time.

"Leave!" she continued to yell into the phone.

"No… no…I can't," I whispered.

"And why the hell not."

"Didn't you hear what I said about my mother?"

"She don't know where you at. And she don't know where you goin', stupid."

"Look, I don't know when I'll be able to call again. But I'll e-mail you or call," I said, looking at her e-mail address on the card. Then it dawned on me for the first time. Her card read 'Tracey At Your Service'. *Why in the hell would an old ass stripper have a business card*, I thought. At that moment I wondered if anybody in my life was good for me.

"Bitch, don't too many people e-mail no more. That shit is played. Hit me up on MySpace."

"MySpace? I don't have an account."

"Get one, bitch!" Tracey said, hanging up in my ear.

"No problem," I responded, like I was ending my business call.

Ms. Dottie was back in the doorway again, so I had to play it off. She gave me a smug look and snatched her pink slip back outta my hand.

"Your phone time is from 8 a.m. to 9 a.m., and from 5 p.m. to 6 p.m. Learn the rules," she gritted through her teeth, then walked away.

Wthin seconds, I was on my way back to my bedroom. "I gotta hurry up and get out of this damn place," I said to myself, just before Cat walked by and bumped me on purpose. We stopped and looked at each other for a few seconds, before she turned around and walked away displaying a huge grin. "What the fuck is wrong with these bitches around here?" I said, as I turned back around. *I hope this prostitute shit works out.*

Chapter Eight

The next night arrived quicker than I could handle. I looked out of my bedroom window, while I squirmed and finally squeezed into my tight fitting pants, still amazed at the cars coming through the gate. About four SUVs rolled up like the president was coming. As the drivers hopped out and opened the doors for their celebrities for the evening, my jaw dropped. I had never seen anything like that before. One by one, the blinged-out dudes entered the house, as more cars followed. By the time I was completely dressed, I peeped back out the window one last time, only to see that a Hummer, a few exotic cars, and a white stretch Escalade had been added to the list.

The clock read midnight, which meant I needed to get my ass downstairs. I hesitantly walked out of the room, while tightening the sparkling belt around my waist. Ms. Dottie had decided on a pair of tight gold-colored spandex pants to accent my ass. She said since I was new, the fellas could smell new booty, and would want the more experienced girls, so I'd have to really make them want me. I felt like my outfit would do the trick. I was feeling good about the way I looked: not too trashy, but sexy enough to have a big-tymer bite the bait.

The moment I hit the bottom step, I grabbed a glass of champagne off the waiter's tray. He had three glasses left, and on the real, I needed all three. I sipped my drink, nodded at two of the bodyguards Daddy hired to protect us, and moved closer to the showroom. Instantly, a few eyes shot my way. They were potentials, but didn't look like much to me. The place was packed like a club on a Friday night, so I figured there were more choices to come.

Several guys lined the wall in the hallway, just kicking it, while most of the girls hung out in the showroom, attacking their prey. My eyes floated back and forth, not recognizing one familiar face. I thought I would see popular people- MTV type niggas. But all I saw were big chains, iced out jewelry, and plenty of nobodys.

I put on my game face, making sure I didn't look like a newbie as I strutted across the room real sexy-like. But deep inside, I was scared to death. *Slow Motion*, by Juvenille rocked through the speakers, and was perfect for setting the mood. I hummed the lyrics just a bit until I spotted Cat out of the corner of my eye.

She sat on some guy's lap with her legs wrapped around his waist. Cat straddled him frontward, like she'd known him for years. He laughed and joked, while groping her breasts at the same time. He must've been somebody big, 'cause another muscular guy stood behind his chair, like he was only interested in his safety. *A Bodyguard?* If so, he wasn't easy to deal with. I smiled at the huge man, but all I got was a slight grin in return. No, can you come here, no finger movements...nothing. I had to get somebody's attention, or Ms. Dottie was gonna have my ass thrown out the next morning.

Continuing to prance around the room, I finally heard

a faint voice from behind. "What's up, sexy?" the voice asked.

I turned to see a chubby pale-skinned guy, who looked like he'd O-g'd, *way too much gold*. He had more chains than Mr. T., and matching teeth to go along with them. He guzzled down a Corona, while looking directly at my breasts. I knew they were perky, but damn, he was mesmerized.

I played with my freshly done hair, which was placed behind each of my ears. Nervously, I pulled a few strands to the front, and did a sexy dance to the beat of the music, while pretending to be in my element. I could've sworn they were playing the same song over and over again, especially when I heard, "Umm...I like it like that. Slow motion baby...." It didn't matter though, the music was fitting.

"Hey sexy," I said, in a faint voice.

"Yo, Ma. That gold sho look good on you," he uttered.

"Oh, yeahhhhhh." I let my syllables drag. "Those chains look good on you," I responded. I looked around the room to see who was watching me. Nobody. All I saw were girls going in for the kill. They were boosting egos, feeling, licking, and doing whatever necessary to get the guys to go to their rooms. I took notes, and pulled my chain lover closer to me.

"So, you like what you see?" I asked.

"That depends."

I wasn't expecting those words, and couldn't really think about what to say next. "What's your name, cutie?" I smiled.

"What's my name?" He stepped back. "Yo, don't you watch videos? Besides, where the fuck you been lately?

I'm the shit!"

Obviously, he was pissed with me, and decided to get extra loud. His lips puckered after he snarled at me a few more times. Ms. Dottie was already on it, and sent School Teacher over to smooth things over. She wrapped her left arm around his neck gently, and massaged his dick with her left hand, while he continued to go off. I took my cue and backed away slowly.

"You a'ight?" one of our bodyguards asked me.

"I'm good," I responded, with an embarrassing look on my face.

"I'm Drake. If you need me, holla. Literally," he joked.

I thanked Drake. He winked, leaving me open for the next potential. Strangely, he was the cutest thing in the room.

Cinnamon walked over to me on her way to grab some finger sandwiches. She clutched my arm and asked what happened with me and Tut. When I asked who in the hell was Tut, she just laughed. She gave me the quick run down on how the dude I'd just insulted was named Tut. The new wonder in the music business. He had the #1 record on the Billboard charts, and was about to be signed by G. Rock, the owner of his own independent label. When she pointed to G. Rock, I felt like crying. Cat was with G. Rock, and at that point, grindin' all over his dick, and caressing his muscular arms. G. Rock was who I needed. Big Money and a one-shot deal.

At that moment, I recognized a familiar face walking into the showroom as Cinnamon walked away. It was Truman, a popular R&B singer. All the available girls circled him. Luscious, one of the white girls, did a hand stand, and opened her legs wide, only to close them by wrapping them around his neck. Damn, I didn't stand a chance, 'cause the competition was thick. Every chick in the room had their own niche, and I had to find one quick. I needed game and fast. Out of my league, I didn't know which way to turn. My focus was on the one thing I desired most...dead presidents.

I stood motionless for a minute, kinda star struck in my own way. Cinnamon passed by and handed me a glass of Patron. I wasn't normally into the hard stuff, but I needed it. I tilted my chin all the way back, and took the double shot straight to the head.

I searched the room for a waiter with more drinks. For some strange reason, every black and white tuxedo seemed to be headed in the opposite direction. I smoothed my hair down when I realized what was going on. It was the boss man. When Daddy was in the house, all hailed to the King. Daddy's reputation superseded his name. He was known to pay well, and everybody wanted to be a part of his empire. All the major players in the room made contact with him somehow. The attention proved his level of stardom.

I watched Daddy closely, amazed at the way people admired him. I was starting to feel the effects of my drinks, when suddenly I felt a pair of eyes watching me just as closely as I watched Daddy. I caught a glimpse of my short, muscular admirer staring at me from across the room. I turned my head 'cause I didn't want him thinking that I wanted him, nor did I want a beef with the trick who was trickin' up on him. I guess, I should've, 'cause money was the name of the game around here, and Daddy made it clear, a lot needed to be made tonight. So what if

I had to fight Cat for G. Rock.

I responded to every one of G. Rock's gestures he made behind Cat's back. He licked out his tongue like a snake, I did the same. He kissed on Cat's neck, while eyeing me down. In return, I licked my finger and rubbed my nipples in a circular motion. Emotions ran deep and the alcohol took over. I was starting to really dig dude. Suddenly, he pushed Cat from his lap, stood, and walked toward me. Both of his boys followed, all with a thuggish strut. Cat stood behind them, wondering where she went wrong. By her expression, I knew I'd pay for stealing her paycheck later.

The moment G. Rock walked up to me, he grabbed my hand, and squeezed it tightly. I was expecting him to kiss it, but the look in his eyes told me he was a rough-neck, so kissing was out. He snapped his fingers, and his boy grabbed two glasses of bubbly. The good bubbly, the kind I was used to drinking with Rich.

After just a few quick sips, G. Rock's game was real believable. He talked a little about how he was this and that, and how he wanted me to be his #1 side-chick. I laughed, and rubbed on him just as I'd seen Cat do. He was slightly shorter than me, which was a turn off. I liked my men big. But G. Rock's muscles were enough to get me through the night, especially the way his t-shirt sculpted his chest. The more comfortable I got, the closer I got to him, and mocked what I'd seen with the other girls. I licked the side of his face, enticing him to make a move.

Finally, he moved aside, and held out his hand, motioning me to lead the way. For a moment, I thought his big-ass bodyguard was coming with us, until I saw Sushi grab him by the hand and place it on the lower part of her waist. She winked at me, and exited the room.

When we approached the bottom of the steps, Ms. Dottie shot me an approving look, and nodded. I guess I had finally impressed her. G. Rock held me by the waist and pressed his body close to mine, following me all the way to my room, smelling like a barrel of Hen-Dog.

As soon as we entered my room, G. Rock went ballistic. He yanked his shirt above his shoulders and tossed it across the room like a mad-man. He stood muscle bound, with his shoulders hunched, staring at me like he was in the ring with his opponent. His reddish colored eyes revealed he was drunk and ready for attack. When his jeans dropped to his knees, and the sound of his huge belt buckle sounded, I snapped. What was I doing? I needed to leave.

I headed toward the door at full speed, still fully dressed. By the time my hand touched the handle, the strength in his arms had come in handy. He grabbed me from underneath my stomach, and pulled me back forcefully, lifting me into mid-air. He never made a sound, but his lips got busy. He sucked from the nape of my neck, down to the crease of my back. The ripping sound of my shirt confirmed that I was done. There was no turning back. My C cups released into the air, while G. Rock undressed the rest of me, like he was paid to steal the clothes off my back. His attack wasn't what I expected for my first time. I'd fucked plenty of dudes in my years before Rich without really caring about them, but at least we pretended things were gonna go somewhere. This was so different, different and scary. I immediately thought about catching some disease, or even AIDS, so I tried to push G. Rock off of me to grab a condom, but his strength was too much and overpowering.

"I...gottttttta get a condom," I moaned from under-neath, while he had me pinned.

G. Rock ignored me. He was in his own world. I knew I had to get serious.

"Daddy, won't be happy." I pushed at his chest. "He said we have to use condoms, so I don't wanna have to tell him that you wouldn't let me get the damn thing out the drawer!"

G. Rock looked at me in shock. "You cursing at me?" His face frowned.

"No, sweetie. I wanna respect Daddy's house. On the real. He gets crazy when we don't listen."

"If the big man insists," G. Rock said, letting up just enough for me to slide from underneath and stand to my feet. I walked to the dresser to grab a condom, while he fondled me the whole way, and never let go of my breasts.

Suddenly, I felt the sensations of what he was doing, but had mixed emotions. My insides were beginning to moisten, which was good for me, 'cause I needed things to go quickly and smoothly. But every time, I tried to really get into the foreplay, I wanted to throw up. G. Rock paused shortly, just enough to slip the condom on, and was back on the job. Now he moved with even more speed. The closer he came to penetration, the more I gagged. His aggressive movements told me he wasn't about to take things slow like I needed him to. He wanted something to jump off instantly.

Suddenly, he stepped up his aggressive erotic tactics a notch. He yanked me by my hair and slammed me back down onto the bed. Flat on my back, I laid as his body lunged down on me. This time, no kisses, no rubbing, no warning. He entered me rough and rugged-like, and with speed. No drink in the world could have prepared me. G. Rock didn't waste any time. He pounded hard and energetically like a raging bull. *Damn, it can't go in any deeper,* I thought. He was giving me his all. He pumped in and out like he was near explosion. I closed my eyes, thinking it would only be a quickie. Wrong!

G. Rock lifted his body above me, and threw my legs over his shoulders. A new-found energy filled his eyes. "Damn, you got soft skin," he moaned. His tongue licked the sides of my legs like a wild beast. Then once again, he drilled me. I held on for dear life while the bed made a loud squeaky noise, and rocked up and down.

In and out he pounded for nearly five minutes. I just laid there and pretended like it wasn't happening. Before long, any wetness I had conjured up was gone. I was as dry as the Sahara desert, and G. Rock's dick felt like a hot, dry stone scraping against the sands. It was painful, yet I was more concerned about when it would all end. The Patron had my head spinning as it was being banged against the bed, but it wasn't enough to make me believe this was okay.

Suddenly, my big break came. G. Rock's body shook as he drained the backed-up pipe, but somehow his dick didn't deflate all the way. The crazy bastard still managed to beat my pussy like a drum. He gripped the side of my legs with force, ready for his nut. Quickly, I lifted my ass upward, off the bed just a bit, to keep from needing a hysterectomy the next morning. I closed my eyes and groaned along with him.

It was the longest groan, I'd ever experienced.

"Ohhhhhhhhhhhh!" we yelled together.

"Hell yeah!" he shouted, as he quickly snatched off the condom and released all over my stomach. My eyes closed instantly. I was mad as hell, but relieved that it was over.

Twenty minutes later, I struggled to get up to see my client to the door.

"Let's hook up, again," G. Rock suggested, trying to sneak one last kiss on my neck.

"I'd like that," I lied.

"Shit...I might be back tonight."

He grinned proudly when he left, like he'd done something spectacular. I had already rated him a seven, and gave myself a two for not throwing up all over the place. I was supposed to shower, and be back downstairs on duty, but I couldn't. The mirror was calling me. I wanted to take a look at myself, but was afraid of what I would see, what I had become. I felt like I had hit an even lower point in life, selling my body just for safety and a little bit of cash. If Ms. Dottie or Daddy wasn't satisfied with my performance, they could kick me out.

I didn't give a fuck, I needed a moment.

I sat on the edge of the bed and slipped my red silk robe on. With my hands cradling my face, I thought about how I had gotten myself in this situation. The thought of my mother startled me. She was probably looking for me at this very moment. With the excitement, and anticipation of how my first night on duty would turn out, I allowed it to slip my mind.

The loud triple knock on the door frightened me. Ms. Dottie didn't knock that way. Oh shit! It was probably G. Rock. He said he might come back. *I just thought he was talking shit.* I dropped my robe to the floor, and hurried to grab my clothes. The knocks continued, and then a voice spoke. It was Daddy's voice. *Oh, shit, I'm in trouble,* I thought.

I slid my left leg into my pants and hopped to the door, trying to get the other one inside the pant leg. All of a sudden, the door swung open, and Daddy was standing there with a mean look on his face.

"When I knock, you open," he said firmly. No smiles were cracked.

I shook my head in fear.

He shut the door behind him and walked closer to me. Instinct told me to back up slowly. "So, how'd it go?" he asked, with concern.

"Uuuuh...I guess it went okay," I stuttered, unsure if G. Rock told him that I laid there like a dead bug.

"Sit down, we need to talk," he ordered.

"'Bout what?" I tried to keep my face from wrinkling, 'cause I was scared as hell.

He kept it real vague, which made things worse. "About your work around here." His eyebrows twitched. "I think everything is gonna be good." He smiled slightly. "G. Rock seems to be happy. He wants to send his boy up for another thousand. You good with that?"

I wanted to say hell no, instead I said, "Oh yeah, it's cool."

"That's a good girl," he replied, slapping me on the leg. "You're gonna be that fiyah around here. I can feel it."

I smiled, accepting the comment, but knowing deep inside, it was an insult. I was better than this, but my situation had me hostage.

"Where you from?" he asked.

"I'm from Jersey...East Orange," I lied.

Daddy shook his head like he approved. "That's cool. I know a few cats up in East Orange. You got family?"

"Nah, not really. You met my cousin, Tracey. She all I got."

"Where's your mother and father? Dead?" he asked, while looking at me with sympathy.

"Yeah," I quickly responded. "My mother died at an early age, so I never really knew her." I tried to look sad.

"Don't worry, baby girl, I'm yo daddy now. I got you. You feel me?"

I smiled. "Yeah, I feel you."

Somehow, I did look at him as a father figure. He was big, confident, and had such an authoritative style about himself that I wanted him to be my daddy. I wanted anyone who could tell me everything would be okay, and that they would protect me forever.

"Now, if you got a man, or a wanna-be man out there somewhere, now is the time to tell me. I had a many niggas come up in here on a beef tip, trying to get their so-called women outta here. I don't go for no bitches bringing trouble to my spot. Ya feel me?"

"Oh, I can assure you, nobody will come claiming me."

"Good. I want you all to myself," he said.

"You got me." I laughed, with my arms wide open. "Nobody wants me for real anyway."

"Why would you say that? You damn sho sexy as hell."

"You know how guys are."

"No, I don't," he responded, with a more serious look.

"Well, are you in a serious relationship?"

"This is funny," he laughed, obviously loosening up with me. "I've never had one of my girls get into my business. But I'ma go 'head and answer that."

"Good," I responded, starting to feel a bit more comfortable.

"Bitches can never be trusted," he said bluntly. "And I'ma let you in on a little secret, I'd kill a bitch for sure, if she cheated on me or even crossed me at all. So it's best that I stay single."

The way he spoke gave me the chills. I knew he meant it from the bottom of his heart. I grabbed my forearms and listened to him spill his guts about women, his distrust mostly. He obviously needed me to listen to him, just like I needed the therapy too. For the next hour, we were like two mental patients, seeking treatment from each other. Before long, Daddy got up, handed me a small stack of money from his pocket, and headed to the door.

"Consider this something extra 'til you get your check next week."

"Thank you, but you don't have to," I said, putting on the charm. I held the money in his direction. I knew exactly how to make a man think I didn't want his money.

"No, it's yours to spend. Candy, sweet Candy," he repeated. He shook his head with pleasure.

I smiled, ready to freshen myself up, and prepare for G. Rock or whoever had next. I was shocked at Daddy's next move.

"Don't worry about tonight," he spoke, with a little hesitance in his voice. "Get some rest. I'll straighten everything with Ms. Dottie and G. Rock. And tomorrow, I want you to go out and get yo'self some gear. Keep this

between us." Daddy nodded. "I don't do this for everybody." He smiled slightly and closed the door behind him.

I was on cloud nine, knowing that my work was done
for the night. Strangely, I was sad to see Daddy go. His
short visit was the highlight of my night, not to mention,
there was something that I liked about his old ass. Maybe
it was the way he smelled...so damn good.

I flipped through the stack of money, happy as hell.
Turns out, the $1000.00 was the most cash I'd held in my
hand in a long time. Daddy had no idea he was starting
something. He knew nothing about my background, how I
used to blow through money, and my plan was to keep it
that way.

Chapter Nine

The next morning it seemed like everyone was up early, sticking to their daily routines, and getting themselves fixed up. After Sushi showed me how to set up a MySpace page, I made my short phone call to Tracey. She cursed me out in both English and Pig Latin for calling her so early in the morning. I tried to explain about my morning phone hours, but Tracey wasn't trying to hear it. I told her we'd meet at noon, at Amy Ruth's on 116th Street. That would give me plenty of time to cop some new gear with a portion of the money Daddy had given me; the rest would be saved for my get-away plan. I knew just the place in lower Manhattan to get the gear that would make Daddy wanna lace me with extra cash every weekend.

I let out a huge sigh when I walked back to my room and saw my door wide open. I was sick of Ms. Dottie, and I'd only been in the house for three days. When I walked inside, I felt someone breathing behind me like a damn dragon. I turned and was hit with an open hand. Slap! *What the fuck,* I thought.

Cat rushed me like she was getting paid by the NFL. She grabbed my neck and placed me in position to be her punching bag. "You thought you was gonna play me. Huh, bitch?"

I stood stiff, trying to figure out how to handle the situation. Meanwhile, her hands went wild as she fought me like a female cat. No punches, no skills, just wild open hand throws. *Now I know how her ass got the name.* I tried not to get too rough with Cat, not wanting to get thrown out, but she was asking for it.

I swung back a few times, but just enough to show her I wasn't a punk. I threw up my hands like a real fighter, ready to go toe to toe Brooklyn style, but she still wanted to do the junior high fighting thing. Although I bobbed and weaved, her long red nails scratched me on my face a few times. Eventually, my arms flew in the air, trying to shield myself from the licks. I decided to fight dirty too. I reached behind and grabbed her by her bad weave. She squirmed, trying to release herself from my grip. I let loose abruptly, and backed up, but she kept swinging into mid-air. When she realized I had maneuvered my body away from her range, she got even madder.

"Word is out, you a cut throat!" she spat.

Sushi heard the commotion and came running like Forest Gump. "Oh…God…no…no…stop!" she yelled.

Sushi's screams got louder, causing more girls to come into the hallway. "Ms. Dot's comin'," I heard one of the girls say. Cat stopped abruptly, and took a few hits from me just to set me up. I was too stupid to realize what was going on.

When Ms. Dottie showed up in front of the doorway, I was on my last punch. Caught dead in the act, it looked like I was the one who initiated the fight. Cat held her hands in the air, and played the dumb role. The bitch was surrendering, but only after she'd scratched the hell out of my face. We both had blood on our hands, but she definitely got the best of me. I did, however, have a plug of her weave in my palm to show that I'd put in work.

"What's this all about?" Ms. Dottie asked walking into my room.

"Hell if I know!" Cat responded.

"Umm huh," Ms. Dottie mumbled. "Then why are you in Candy's room?"

I cringed at the sound of my new name. Cat shrugged her shoulders. Then grinned at me like she'd won the battle.

"Both of you, downstairs," Ms. Dottie ordered. "This is the only free time you got! I suggest you use it wisely," she snapped, walking toward us, backing us both in the direction of the staircase.

I continued to walk backward, watching Cat's every move from the corner of my eye. Even though Ms. Dottie was front and center, I still didn't trust Cat. She was the anything goes type of broad, so I had to be ready.

When I hit the bottom step, Sushi was standing there with tears in her eyes, like she was the one who got beat down. "Oh, me Candy, look at your pretty face," she said.

I moved away slowly. She might've been out to get me too.

"Oh, I'm fine. Real fine," I repeated, making sure Cat could hear the confidence in my voice.

"You have scratch on you face."

Sushi was cool, but the moment she touched my face, I moved her hand. Ms. Dottie, in return, hit me with a nasty look.

"I'm straight, Sushi. Don't worry about me. On the

real, I'm from the hood. I just try not to act like it. I've been through worse."

"Hood?" Sushi asked, with a confused expression.

I let out a slight laugh. "Never mind, Sushi. I gotta go. We'll talk later."

"Oh, me too," she said, grabbing my hand again. She was way too touchy feely for me, but I knew it was a part of her culture. I just wish somebody would teach her that black folks needed space.

"Sushi, I'll be back."

"No…please…please…I go. We have girl fun," she said, grabbing my arm. She grinned so hard, I didn't have the heart to hurt her feelings.

"Umm…here you go," Ms. Dottie said, interrupting us.

As soon as I looked at the pink slip of paper, I knew exactly what it was. However, my eyes almost popped out of my head when I looked at the $350.00 fine.

"Ms. Dottie, it wasn't even my fault. Cat started it," I pleaded.

She looked at me like I was crazy. "I don't care who started it. We don't tolerate that ghetto shit up in Daddy's House, so like I said earlier, I suggest you find something else to do with your time when you're not on your back. Moving right along," she said, before checking something off on her clipboard then walked away.

"I'm never gonna make any money in this house," I said, before balling up the pink slip of paper and throwing it across the room.

"Oh, don't worry, you make lots," Sushi replied, with a huge smile.

I didn't know how I was gonna explain to Tracey that

I'd brought an Asian chick along for our lunch date, and a poorly dressed one at that. I started to tell Sushi that she had to change out of that skin-tight leopard leotard before we left, but I laid low. I had already had enough controversy for one day.

Within an hour, me and Sushi had caught one cab, and several trains to all my old shopping spots. I hadn't shopped in the city in years, but managed to find all the fly shit with the little bit of money I had. My expensive taste in clothes had been somewhat tamed over the last year, but it was still there, just buried deep inside. I wanted badly to rock Chanel, Prada, and my favorite, Christian Dior. Instead, I got the next best thing. I got two pair of jeans from a boutique in Soho, which looked like they cost a mint. I also picked up a few jazzy shirts that had an expensive appearance.

I was starting to feel like the old Candice again. I walked from store front to store front window shopping like I was living a normal life again. Every now and then, a loud noise would spark my attention, and a Crown Vic passing by would scare the shit outta me and take me back to reality. A reality that told me that I could never get too comfortable. I was already on edge hoping that whoever was after me back in Jersey would never find me in Long Island. My new residence seemed to be pretty safe. The minute we passed a Sunglass Hut, I smiled. I had to go in. The pair of Christian Dior shades in the window had my name all over them. Me and Sushi went inside, and ten minutes later, I came out rockin' a pair of $320.00 shades.

After looking in a few more stores, it was close to noon, so we headed to the restaurant to meet Tracey. When we got there, the lengthy line had me heated. Seconds later, Tracey pulled up with Luke, and hopped out of the car like a celebrity walking the red carpet. Luke just shot me a fake wave, like he wasn't interested in my well being anymore, and scurried off on two wheels. Tracey switched to the front door, whispered something in the guy's ear, who was obviously in charge of the waiting list for the restaurant, and within two short minutes, we were next to be seated. She nodded to me in the line proudly, until she realized Sushi was with me.

"Who the fuck is this?" Tracey asked.

"Oh, this is Sushi. She lives with me at the house. She's mad cool." I smiled.

"Bitch, we link up, and you bring some hooker wit' you? With a fuckin' nose ring. You don' lost yo' damn mind."

Sushi never said a word, but her expression said it all. She wasn't about to get buck with Tracey, who was look- ing crazy with a fake leopard print fur shawl thrown across her shoulder, and black thigh high patent leather boots to match.

"We got some juicy shit to talk 'bout. I'on think we need no damn outsider's company," Tracey replied. "Especially no fried rice eatin' muthafuckas."

"On the real, it's okay," I pleaded, with my eyes. Sushi was my only ally at the house, besides Cinnamon, who I didn't really know too well, so I wanted to stay on good terms with her.

"C'mon damn it," Tracey finally said, blowing breath through her lips, and opening the door.

"I told you it would be okay," I whispered to Sushi.

We followed the male host to our table located way in the back of the restaurant, which was perfect, since Tracey had something juicy to tell me. I prayed it was about my mother's whereabouts. We sat down, grabbed our menus, and made small talk, while trying to decide what to eat.

"Candy, they no have noodles," Sushi blurted out.

"Who the fuck is Candy?" Tracey snapped.

"She Candy." Sushi pointed to me with a big smile.

"Maybe this was all a bad idea." Tracey rolled her eyes. "I'ma have to talk to Luke about this shit. All these fuckin' weirdos and shit." She looked Sushi straight in the eye, but Sushi wouldn't look back, she just sang some unknown Asian song.

Tracey just stared into Sushi's face, ranting and yelling obscenities in between her singing. After cursing for the fiftieth time, Tracey smacked, "You better shut the fuck up if you gonna stay at this table!"

Before long the waiter came over, ready to take our order. Tracey was so caught up into telling me that she really needed to talk to me alone, that I couldn't even order my food. I knew something serious had to be wrong.

"Tell me now," I pressed. "What is it? Is it Velma?"

"Give me a #8," Tracey said to the waiter.

"And you Miss?" he asked me.

I couldn't speak. "Tell me, Tracey." I panicked.

Tracey continued to ignore me and decided to order for me. "Chicken and Waffles for her, and Chow Mein for her." She pointed at Sushi, and laughed loud enough to have everyone looking at our table.

"We don't have Chow Mein. Only what's on the menu," the waiter said sarcastically.

"I know that shit, damn it. Don't get smart, 'cause your tip just got shorter."

The waiter walked away and I got close up into Tracey's face. "Is she really out? 'Cause I saw it on the computer with my own eyes. I just want one person to confirm that they've seen her."

"I'm not a hundred percent sure. If you hadn't of brought your lil' friend, we could rap. You know, go visit a few peeps who really know what's goin' on. "

I scooted my chair over so Sushi couldn't hear. "Tell me now. I gotta know."

"Well, Uncle Cedric called Mike about an hour ago and said …"

Sushi abruptly started singing Rick James' *Super Freak* at the table. Tracey went ballistic. She jumped up and scooted Sushi's chair from underneath her bottom. "Get up!" she instructed.

"Where we go?" Sushi asked, with a puzzled look.

"We? No, you. Let's go." Tracey pulled Sushi by the hand and led her to the front door. "You wait here. I'ma tell'em to bring yo damn food right here. I need to talk to my cuz in peace. You got me?"

Sushi nodded with confusion. I stood up and looked on long enough to see that she was okay and watched as Tracey headed back to the table. The minute we sat back down, I started drilling. With my neck stuck out like a giraffe, I asked, "What did Uncle Cedric say? I gotta know, and who the fuck is this Mike you were talking about?"

"Oh, don't worry about him. It's just some cat I know. Anyway, don't hold me to this, but Cedric said Ray called him from jail and ummm…"

"Ummm…what?" I edged.

"Ray said she's out for sure. But not lookin' for you."

"You believe that!"

"If Ray said it, it's official. He's the only honorable member left in the family. I'm not really sure about any-thing else that was said. Just don't come by my spot. You know…just in case. I'm supposed to go see Cedric later to get the rest of the story. He already told me bits and pieces, but mostly gossip. I wanna hear the real deal."

"I'm going too."

"Hell to da naw!"

"Why not?" I begged.

"Lay low for a while. I don't even wanna talk to you for a sec, so I don't have to tell Aunt V no lies. Hit me up on MySpace in the meantime." She smiled, showing those awful gold teeth. It was a fake smile, trying to make me believe everything would be okay. "I saw your message this morning. I responded to it," she added. "Your page is cute."

"Who cares about that at a time like this," I said, in a panicky voice. "You know how coldhearted she is. How could the feds let this happen? She's a damn menace to society."

"You should'a testified against her ass, and then she wouldn't be out. Now you like fish grease…hot," she joked, licking her lips.

"On the real, Tracey, this is serious. No time for jokes."

"I'm dead serious." She laughed.

For some reason, I felt like there was something Tracey wasn't telling me. I knew there was always a strong possibility that my mother would get out, that's why my testimony was so important. After all, cases have to be built by the defense. We were all snitching on one another, but I knew I deserved to be free. I was forced into the business through my blood. That should've gotten my mother ten years by itself.

Nobody in our crew knew what I knew. They felt like if I was getting the money alongside Big V, I should'a done the time alongside her too. The entire family was against me. It didn't matter though. If I could help it, I wouldn't be strong armed by Big V. *I gotta get in touch with Agent Barnes*, I thought, as the food arrived at the table.

I pushed my chicken and waffles to the side. My appetite was shot. My only concern was making sure my mother wouldn't have her freedom for long.

Chapter Ten

Rich's black Dodge Magnum pulled up to Tracey's joint like we were on a stake out. When the car finally came to a damn stop, I jumped out like I was ready for some shit to go down.

"Big V," Rich called out to me.

"What, mufucka!" I turned my neck all the way around like the damn exorcist. "Go 'head and tell everybody my damn name."

I bent down to fix the handmade cuff I had put in my jeans, while looking around to check my surroundings. I felt like a teenager trapped in a thirty-six year old body. My form-fitted jeans clutched to my firm hips. I'd been pumping iron in the pen, so I was shapelier than ever.

"You know which building?" Rich whispered, through the window.

"I got this," I snapped.

"Don't do nothin' crazy."

"You should'a told your lil' girlfriend that a long time ago," I responded, reading the building numbers. I laughed crazily.

"Shit, you know how I feel about your girl. I don't get along wit' snitches," Rich responded.

"Nigga, stop lyin'. You still in love," I added, swiftly walking away.

Rich's eyes followed me into Tracey's building, but he didn't dare get out. I didn't need no help. Tracey could be handled without back-up. Just in case anything went down, I had already told him to pull off and meet me at my boy's place on Lenox Ave.

I passed two young boys dressed in black hoodies on my way in. I gave 'em both a nod, since they were lookin' like they wanted to try their hand. I was fresh outta prison, but still looked young, and good enough to get a few stares. Just in case they had me fooled, or any other foolish thoughts on the brain, I held my hand inside my shirt and made a bulky shape, symbolizin' a gun.

"What up, baby girl?" one of the guys called out.

"Shut the fuck up," I barked. Our eyes met, and I stared them down hard. Real hard.

Finally, they backed down and made their way in the other direction. They knew I meant business. Instantly, I proceeded to look for Tracey's apartment number. I knew the information I'd been given was accurate, because my snitch wouldn't want to see me again if anything he told me turned out to be false.

My feet moved cautiously, while my eyes watched over my shoulder for anything behind me. It only took a few seconds before I spotted Tracey's door. "29E, jack-pot," I said out loud. My snitch was always on point. Shit, he valued his life too much not to be. I pulled out the small jimmy from my side, and popped the cheap-ass locks. It was easier than I thought.

The door squeaked like some shit out of a haunted house. I peeked around slowly, before stepping completely inside. Once realizing Tracey wasn't home, I quickened my pace. There was no need in trashing the place, 'cause there was enough shit thrown around to have the place condemned.

Out the left side of my eye, I caught an image that gave me mixed emotions. The picture of my sister, Vicki, Tracey's mother, stared me in my face. She knew my style, and knew my intent. Quickly, I pushed the frame downward, no longer allowing her to peep my moves. Besides, there was no time for emotional shit.

I started to look for anything I could find. I pulled out all the drawers to her plastic storage bin, but found nothin'. Nothin' but a bunch of damn bills. I flipped over every pillow, Snicker's wrapper and dirty-ass condom in sight. *My niece ain't nothin' but a nasty hoe*, I thought, as I began to get pissed off.

Surprisingly, Tracey's computer was still on to the left of me, which caught my attention, because of the explicit photos on the screen. It was Tracey's MySpace page. I couldn't help but wonder how many times she'd been on that thing contacting Candice throughout the day. My brother, Ray, had already passed word that Tracey talked to my daughter frequently via that MySpace shit. I rushed to the keyboard, ready to punch a few keys. I hoped it was still active, so I could send my baby a message.

Surprised by the sudden sounds of the front door opening, I backed away from the computer and turned to face what was before me. When Tracey walked in, I could'a bought her ass for a penny. She stood at the door with her bottom lip hung low. She had one hand on the knob, and the other on her hip. I wondered if was she was still comin' in, or gonna make a run for it.

"Problem?" I questioned.

"Problem? Yeah…I gotta problem a'ight. What da fuck you doin' in my spot?"

She looked me up and down, waitin' for an answer. I couldn't be certain, but her stare hid her fear well. "You questionin' me?"

"Big V, e'erybody ain't afraid of you."

"Then why the fuck you still standin' at the door? Come the fuck in here. I gotta talk to you 'bout something."

"When you get out?" Tracey asked, closing the door slightly, but not all the way . She kept looking back toward the door, like she was expecting somebody to come rushin' in.

"I'm asking the fuckin' questions. Now where's our girl?"

"Our girl? Who?"

I gave her a slight smile. "You know who I'm talkin' 'bout. And shut that damn door. Lock it too," I ordered.

Tracey was up to some shit. I could smell it. Planning my next move, I eyed the bottle of Drano sitting on the floor near Tracey's leg. Not that it was my choice of weapon, but I needed a back-up plan. I let my eyes wander for a moment, wondering how much lay inside, and how potent the liquid was.

Besides, Tracey still hadn't complied and locked the damn door. After giving her a moment, and looking deep into her eyes, I felt her defiance. Quite frankly, it filled the room. I knew she wasn't gonna do as I instructed.

I wasted no time. Two steps and a strong grip later, I had Tracey pinned to the wall by her damn throat. "Where she at, huh?" I taunted. I pushed the door all the way shut with my right hand, and turned the wobbly lock.

"Big V, why the fuck you come up in here disre-spectin' me like that?"

Her bitch-ass was whining like a chump. I hated chumps, and was shamed to say she was my niece. "Disrespectin' you? You the one been on the phone sin-gin' my mufuckin' name. You know I finds out every-thing. You think I'on know."

She looked puzzled. I guess wondering who I was talkin' 'bout. Maybe she'd talked to several people about me. "You run your mouth too much. Cedric told me you called, braggin' bout how you gotta look out for Candice. I know she was here. So where the fuck she at now?"

"I'on know!"

"You'on know," I repeated, applying extra pressure to her neck. One of the benefits of being in and out prison was I could snap a fuckin' neck faster than my victim could scream, 'nooooooooo'. "You either with me or against me. Which is it?" I badgered. My face told her this was it. No matter what she said, I knew the answer. She wasn't down with me. Never was. I kept my tight grip with one hand and reached for the Drano with the other. "This some potent shit," I threatened. "Have you foaming out the mufuckin' mouth."

"Look, Aunt V, I know what Candice did was foul. I told'er. But why you got me in this shit!"

Tracey yelled a few words that I couldn't understand. My response, I just tightened the grip on her neck, and tried to pop the top on the Drano.

"Aunt V, noooooooooo...!" my niece screamed.

Out of nowhere, Tracey slipped a knife from the open-ing in her purse. I looked into her eyes and saw my sister.

She looked so much like my side of the family, but acted nothin' like us. It was in our blood to be loyal. "Oh, so you gon' fuckin' kill me?" I asked, with a hurtful expression. My heart sunk just a bit, totally out of the ordinary. Would I allow my niece to shank me? My flesh and blood?

"C'mon, Aunt V, look how you got me? You got me all in the middle of you and Candice's shit!" she screamed, gripping the shank tightly.

I wasn't one for a lot of talkin', so I grabbed her hand in mid-air. We swayed back and forth, like two dudes at a wrestlin' match. Tracey's force told me she wanted me dead. All I really wanted was the whereabouts of my daughter. I couldn't believe Tracey's will. One slip and I'd be punctured straight in the shoulder blade. We struggled for less than a second more, before the knife was up for grabs. She was a huge girl, but I was bigger and much stronger. My mind wrestled with what my next move would be.

A tear fell from Tracey's eye. Fear? Pain? Triumph? I wasn't sure. But I do know the knife went in deep and hard. I couldn't believe she had me like this. My lids opened wide and my eyes protruded to the size of an eight ball. They remained stuck and my body froze. I couldn't believe this was happenin'. I closed my eyes and cried. *A nasty cry.*

Chapter Eleven

No sooner than me and Sushi made it back to the house, I rushed up to my room, taking two steps at a time. Sushi tried to follow, but I told her I needed some time alone. Luckily, she understood and backed off. The house was unusually quiet for 9 p.m., so the noise from my shopping bags seemed extra loud. I figured I would have some me time in my room, throw all my new clothes across my bed, and think about what Tracey had told me about my mother. Besides, I was tired, and my feet were swollen from all the walking in the city.

When I opened the door, my eyes darted around the room. I stared in horror, and my mouth fell open, full of surprise. The bright red lipstick smeared on the walls and the mirrors sent me into a rage. Instantly, my bags hit the floor, and I walked around looking at how my room had been smashed. Somebody obviously hated me.

When I turned to see toilet tissue spread over the bath- room floor, my feet led me in that direction. The closer I got, the smell intensified. I stood speechless in the mirror, just like a character in the Candy Man movie. The lipstick read, "Slut, if you wanna live-go home." This wasn't the work of Big V. This was a hater.

By now, the smell was all in my nose. My adrenaline was on fire. I looked down into the blood-filled toilet and gagged. A combination of soiled sanitary napkins, and balled up bloody tissue stared me in the face. I flushed, and cupped my nose and mouth at the same time. None of it worked. As the toilet overflowed, the water soaked my shoes and freshly painted toes.

Reacting like a mad woman, I jetted from my room and stomped down the hall, still gagging along the way. My first instinct was to bang on Cat's door until she opened, but after the first two loud clunks, something told me to turn the knob. Bam! It was open. Cat was calmly propped up on the bed in a pink-silk one-piece, like she was prepping for a porno set. I charged at her, ready to finish where we'd left off. Even though she saw me, she was caught off guard by my quick approach.

Before she could get off the bed, I grabbed her by her weave and landed a solid punch to the back of her head. Like Tyson in a heavyweight match, my swift aggressive hit knocked her to the floor. She jumped up, ready to fight back, but my anger, combined with frustration, was too much to handle. She started kicking and fighting wildly, with her arms swinging in the air. Big V had taught me that type of fighting was for whimps. I went postal. I snatched an extension cord from the wall, while she threw lashes at my back. I turned quickly, dove into her torso area, and twisted her arm into a painful position behind her back. The moment I knew I had her, I backed her into the wall.

My animalistic behavior had Cat in shock. Surprisingly, I was in shock too. Most would've thought I was on drugs or some type of crazy steroid, but it was simple. I had something to prove. I was tired of living in fear. Finally, I was able to get her in the perfect position. I wrapped the cord around her neck, and tightened it as much as I could. I grinned, seeing the sign of defeat on her face.

"Get...the fuck...off me!" Cat shouted, in between breaths.

"You gonna pay, 'cause being nice don't work with you," I rambled, really getting the hang of being the torturer for once. "I tried to stay out your way...but noooooooooo...you wanna keep fucking with me," I added, while tightening the extension cord even more.

Cat kept lifting her head, trying to sneak some extra air into her lungs. Nothing was working. I had her where I wanted her.

I heard a few of the girls screaming behind me, but I blacked out. The real me was surfacing. I breathed heavily, trying to calm myself. It wasn't working.

"Let..meeeeeee...goooo. Let..meeeee...gooo," Cat repeated.

"Oh, I'm gonna let you go alright." I yanked her by the arm that was held hostage by my forceful grip, and led her about two yards to her toilet. It was sparkling, the total opposite of mine. I got angrier, and forced her head down into the bowl. The cord had fallen off, but the imprint from the force on her neck was still there. I grinned again as she goggled the water to keep from drowning. My patience was running thin. I lifted her head momentarily, to see the fear in her face, and swiftly dunked her head back in. The bubbling noise made me feel good for once.

"You like toilets, don't you!" Of course I got no

response. "Oh, so you don't have any sarcastic remarks now, do you?" I questioned.

My hand had been gripping Cat's head so tightly over the last three minutes, that my palm was now extra greasy. As my grip loosened, I took her head down for one last dive. By now, I had killed any fight left in her. She was as quiet as a church mouse. The most humble I'd ever seen her. I loved every minute of it.

The sudden sound of keys jiggling, told me my adventure was over. I felt Ms. Dottie's hand on my shoulder, pushing me out of the way. She looked at Cat, who was down on her knees and hovering over the toilet in disgust.

"Get up! This is it!" she yelled. "Time for an emergency meeting." She looked at me and smiled. I wasn't quite sure why. "I've already sent Daddy a text message. He'll be here shortly. I've gotta tell you, Miss Candy, this is not good. I've seen this happen before, and Daddy doesn't tolerate it," she fussed, while writing on her pad. She never looked up again. She just rambled on telling me how the last time this happened, both girls were out the door. "I mean, we've gotta make examples outta people like you. Strangely, we didn't have a problem out of Cat until you came along."

She looked at me real evil-like. Although I turned away, her words cut through me like a sharp knife, just about the same time that she ripped my pink slip from her pad. The moment it touched my skin, I crumbled it up into the palm of my hand.

"Fuck your damn fines. Did you see my room?" I yelled.

She shot me with her hand movement, that showed she didn't care. Palm to the face was her favorite. "Save it for

Daddy. Moving right along," she added.

I rolled my eyes, crossed my arms, and huffed loudly.

"That won't help you at all," she fired back. "Have you ever watched the Apprentice?" she asked.

I thought it was a weird question, but answered with a sarcastic, "No!"

"Just wondering. 'Cause you may need to get packed."

I didn't feed into her shit, but was definitely frightened by the sound of the front door downstairs being closed. Daddy's voice yelling upstairs for Ms. Dottie to come down alone startled me. He was always sweet to me, but I'd heard the stories about how he handled problems in the house...ruthless.

"The two of you can behave yourselves, can't you?"

I looked at Cat, but she turned away. I just nodded and kept my arms folded across my chest.

"Stay in your own rooms, until I call for you," she ordered.

I turned, headed to my room, expecting to hear remarks from Cat. Nothing. Not one sound. Inside my room, I closed the door just enough, leaving it slightly cracked. My goal was to eavesdrop. Nervous about how Daddy would react, I paced the floor.

I removed my clothes, and other accessories from the bag to keep my mind occupied. Seconds turned to minutes...minutes turned to almost a half an hour. Suddenly, through the crack in the door a large figure quickly passed by. It snuck past me, headed in the direction of Cat's room. I didn't see Ms Dottie, but figured she wouldn't be far behind.

I sat on my bed as my heart raced. I just knew it was Daddy, on his way to see Cat, and then me next. My feet led me to the door for a quick snoop. I listened for a slap, but nothing was heard. No arguments, no loud talking, nothing.

After several minutes of total impatience, I gave up and moved toward my window. My fidgety frame of mind had gotten the best of me. Staring out my window, I felt a strange presence. When I turned to my fate, I wasn't sure how to react. Daddy just looked at me, saying nothing. A minute went by before he even made a move. Chillingly, he walked toward my bed with long confident strides, still two yards away from me. His interest in my new clothes seemed out of the ordinary, but at least he left the door wide open. As he moved the fabrics around on the bed, scrutinizing each piece, his scowl remained merciless. Finally, he inhaled with frustration and spoke like a betrayed lover.

"So, this is how you show your gratitude?" His voice was more rugged than I'd ever heard.

"Uhh…it wasn't my fault," I confessed.

Before he could say anything else, my heart raced again. I kept my cool, after seeing Cat walk past the door with two heavy suitcases. I was sure my time was near. I guess this is what Ms. Dottie meant when she asked me if I'd seen the Apprentice. Cat was fired, and I was next.

"These are some sexy pieces," Daddy spoke. "Why don't you model for me?"

I was in no mood for antics. I'd rather be fired on the spot.

He walked smoothly over to the door, and pushed it shut. "I'm your customer," he uttered, then pulled a few hundred dollar bills from his money clip. "Here's a little something for you, come get it," he said, eyeing me like a piece of meat.

I figured the cash would be good, since I was well on my way to being evicted. I guess this would be my last hour at Daddy's House. "Anything in particular?" I asked, with my hand pointing to the outfits.

"The black halter dress," he said briskly.

I turned my back and slipped the dress on quickly, wondering what would happen after I modeled. By the time I turned around, Daddy had pulled a chair to the center of the room and flipped the light switch.

I slipped on my stilettos, and strutted around the room like a runway model for all of ten seconds. I breathed heavily, wondering if my quick show had satisfied him.

"Is that what you think I wanted?" he questioned.

My head moved from right to left, as my anxiety grew.

"I thought that you'd be impressed," I stuttered.

"If you really wanted to impress me, you would've taken her out."

My jaw hung low. I couldn't believe what he'd just said.

Daddy continued in a sort of sick-like tone, "It takes a real woman to turn another woman into a cripple. That's how you get gangsta. That's how you impress me. All that cat and dog fighting ain't worth shit. You could've held her in an uncomfortable position, and fucked with her pressure points, prolonged stress positions, until she cracked."

I just looked at him strangely, not sure whether to stay or run. He seemed a bit deranged.

"Everybody has a secret, what's yours?" he asked, still seated calmly. "I have one."

"It doesn't have anything to do with Lisa, does it?" I

asked.

"Who told you about Lisa?" he barked.

"Not really sure," I spoke quickly. I was smart enough to know it was time to change the subject. "Well just so you know, I don't have any secrets." I walked toward Daddy in an effort to seduce him. I placed my hands on his shoulders as he sat stiffly, hoping he could smell the sweet scent on my neck. "You know, I thought coming here meant I was gonna be escorting political men to functions and social events."

He snickered, which lightened the mood. "Well, we do have a political night. Me and the Mayor real tight," he bragged. "It's coming up soon. Really though…what's your deal, Candy?" He looked up into my eyes.

"What you mean?" I asked, avoiding direct eye contact.

"I mean, why are you really here? Some people are here because they were already stripping. This is a step up, like a promotion for them. And others are here because they been fuckin' since they was twelve. What's your story?"

I just shrugged my shoulders.

"I took you in on the strength of Luke. He tells me you runnin' from some nigga."

My heart raced. "Yeah, an old boyfriend. Nothing I can't handle."

"Tell me why I should let you stay?"

I swallowed hard, and kissed at his neck.

"Dance for me, Candy." Daddy crossed his leg and reared back even more.

I blushed, and moved my hands briskly across his thighs. He seemed pleased. So, at that point, I figured he wanted a show, a real show. I backed up a bit, threw my hands high above my head, and moved to the invisible rhythm created in my head. R. Kelly, my favorite singer, always got me in the mood, so I thought about *12 Play*, one of my favorite songs.

"Oh yeah," he moaned, getting deep into my movements.

I closed my eyes and fantasized what it would be like to be Mrs. Daddy, while I continued with my flexible, seductive moves. With my right foot forward, I pivoted in a circular motion. It was starting to even feel good to me, and sugar-coated what Daddy would do to me. When I started gyrating my hips from side to side, Daddy couldn't control himself. He leaned forward, threw his arms on the side of my hips, and moaned, "Yesssssssss. Sweet Candy!"

His touch gave me the chills. Good chills.

"You know…I lost money by getting rid of Cat." The words sizzled through his salivating tongue.

I kept dancing, not sure how to respond.

"You've gotta make double now," he announced. "Then you can stay."

His words were so sharp, I knew there was no negotiation. I still didn't respond, but I knew I was staying. The agreement was on the table. I'd have to make double what Cat made, to make sure Daddy's loss was covered. I could handle that.

Abruptly, I stopped dancing and moved closer, my body kissing at his chest. He smelled so good, so fresh, not old like most men his age.

My goal was to trick Daddy out of some more of that side cash, 'cause my time around here wasn't promised. I had to survive Ms. Dottie and Daddy, so I could afford to move way across the country. I was done with the east coast forever. Sushi was from Texas, and had already told me she had some good connections there. Plus, I had a secret out West.

I looked down at Daddy, who rested his head on the lower part of my stomach. He pressed his head into me, as if he was in ecstasy. Strangely, he felt good. Real good. I longed to be touched, held by a man. A real man, not the G. Rock type.

Daddy just held on to me tightly, not making any moves. I was starting to enjoy my time with him, and strangely began to love everything about him, or maybe just his ability to protect me. I thought about the way he walked, his cool style, his power, and all of it had me twisted all of a sudden. I wanted him. And apparently, he wanted me too.

Daddy had managed to slip his hand up my dress, and was now fully caressing my ass. The feel of his warm hands drove me insane. As fast as I could, I lifted my leg about three inches off the ground, forcing his hand closer to my good stuff. Whether he bit or not, I wanted him to know I was game.

My next move even shocked Daddy. When my lips attacked his large juicy lips, he flinched. For me, the chemistry seemed so real.

Suddenly, Daddy stood up, and moved two steps away from me. I watched him as he headed toward the door quickly. My guess to make sure it was locked.

"I can't get down with the talent," he said, opening the door. "It's one of my oldest rules." He looked at me sadly, as if he really wanted to stay.

I never said a word, just stood there in shock; more like embarrassed. The moment the door shut, I moved closer, and leaned against it, just hoping he would return. He never came back.

Daddy's House

Chapter Twelve

The next day came fast, too fast. Ms. Dottie must've gotten word about my new quota, 'cause she hollered at me in the middle of another boring-ass emergency meeting about not getting to my hair appointment on time. I hadn't even been in the house for a month yet, and I was already sick of the worthless meetings.

"I'm on my way in a sec," I huffed.

"Oh...so you on your way," she countered, writing something on her clipboard. "That's not good enough. You should'a been there!" She looked at her watch. "I told you to see Claude by twelve, and to look your best all day."

"All day?" I questioned. My face twisted up into a knot real quick. Then I contemplated my fate. *I could always leave...live on the streets...stay on the run*, I thought. Then decided against it.

My arm changed positions on the couch. I was getting more comfortable, instead of heading to the back of the house like she instructed, and I know that pissed her off. I scanned the room, noticing the other girls watching me from the corner of their eyes. Most·were hatin'. I could feel it. But some just couldn't believe how I was starting to handle Ms. Dottie. *Is she really expecting me to contin-*

ue to jump as soon as her ass says something? That shit is getting real old.

"Cat's gone now. So the pressure is on," Cinnamon commented to us all. "We gotta make this money."

"That's right," Ms. Dottie said, pulling a stack of white envelopes from her bag. "Last week's pay was good for some, but not all. You'll see when you take a look at your cash." She passed out the envelopes, and one-by-one the complaints started.

"What the fuck you do?" Sushi blurted out.

"Oh, you got three deductions, Sushi. Check your statement. Fine #1- still hogging the gym. Fine #2- Misuse of phone time. And Fine #3- disrespecting me at the last meeting." She grinned devilishy. "That's two hundred in fines."

By the time I had opened my envelope, two other people jumped up with complaints, because their money was short as well. Even though my cash was $350.00 short, I smiled. They obviously had decided to charge me for beating Cat's ass. It was my first time on the payroll since I'd been in the house, and my first big pay date since I'd departed from my mother. My twelve hour days at Texaco didn't pay shit.

When I signed up for this slutty-ass gig, Ms. Dottie told me I'd make thirty percent of the money I brought in. I wasn't sure what kind of calculations they had done, 'cause it seemed like they were pencil whipping me by the looks of the statement, but something was better than nothing.

As soon as Ms. Dottie announced the meeting was over, I made my way toward the hair salon. Out of the blue, a new face caught my attention. A young white chick, who looked to be in her late teens, was being drilled with questions by my good friend, Dr. Charles. The asshole had the same black doctor's bag he carried when he did his finger assault move on me.

I watched as the girl twirled her hair with her index finger, giving off one seductive laugh after another. She was either trying to charm him, or get charmed. Little did she know he was a rapist with a doctor's degree. Then she got hit with a big surprise. Ms. Dottie walked up on her like the police.

"You haven't even been officially hired yet, and you flirting with the damn doctor."

"Ahh...ahh...we were just talking," the young girl replied.

"Yeah, I know," Ms. Dottie countered.

"I was just waiting for her to be assigned a room. Wasn't sure if you had a free bed," Dr. Charles added.

"You got that right," Ms. Dottie bragged. "An empty bed means we're losing money. Gotta keep'em coming. Just so happens, Ms. Candy here helped you get a spot young lady," she said sarcastically. "So thank her."

I was caught off guard, 'cause I was supposed to just be passing by, pretending like I wasn't paying attention to their conversation.

"Candice meet Jordan. Jordan meet Candice," Ms. Dottie said.

To my surprise, the girl had good manners.

"Jordan DeVaughn," she said, giving me her first and last name. I started to say Danielle Crouch, using the name I'd used in the witness protection program, but quickly decided against it. Besides, Ms. Dottie didn't know who Danielle Crouch was anyway, so saying that would've definitely put her ass in question mode. I gave the white girl a smile, and shot the doc a disapproving stare. His weird-ass just winked at me.

"Alright, Candy, that's enough socializing. Go get dolled up," Ms. Dottie ordered.

I marched past them, and headed for an hour of having my hair washed and curled to perfection. The hair-dresser, for some reason, wanted me to look fabulous. He said he'd gotten word that I was gonna be the top girl around the house soon, and I guess he'd heard right. Now with Cat gone, I was the TPIC-Top Pussy In Charge.

By the time my makeover was complete, the other girls had seen eight guys already. Things were pumping, as Daddy would say, and cash was filing in the door. I knew I had to out-do them all, so snagging the next big fish to come through the door wasn't an option.

I went to the showroom and plopped down in the chair, waiting for the next John to arrive, when Sushi offered me a drink. I didn't normally drink in the middle of the day, but I took it. I needed something to calm my nerves, and prepare me for the waiting game.

Just as I downed my drink, a brother was escorted to the showroom. He stood about 5'7, and looked like he hadn't shaved in days. I stood up, ready to go for it, since my only competition was Sushi, Cinnamon and the new girl, Jordan, who was shaking her ass like crazy. All the other girls were upstairs with Johns they'd snagged earlier.

Even though I was the only one standing, he walked around the room, surveying us like new cars. I looked down at his Tims and baggy pants, thinking he might want Sushi. He looked like a rough neck, ready to snatch one of Sushi's body piercings out in the heat of the moment.

Wrong. He stood over Sushi's chair, then moved straight in the direction of the new girl. The size of her eyes doubled.

"This the only white chick you got?" he asked Ms. Dottie.

"For now," she answered, like it was killing her to have patience.

"She'll do. Lead the way," he replied.

Damn, her ass hasn't even been here a day and she's getting picked already. However, I sat back down, thankful that it wasn't me. He had no class, no style, and probably no real money. It took another half an hour before the next potential showed up. I couldn't see what he looked like, 'cause my back was turned, with my face buried in the Sister to Sister Magazine. I lifted my head just a bit, and noticed the ladies' faces seemed to be brighter than before. The momentum had quickly picked up for some reason.

"Ladies, you know the drill," Ms. Dottie said with authority. "Stand up," she ordered, raising her hand.

I wasn't sure what to do, so I followed the other girls. It took me only a second to realize they were lining up, and striking their sexiest next top model poses. *What the fuck?* We didn't normally do this shit when individual men came into the room.

I looked over to see a dark-skinned man pimping

around the room with a humongous white fury kango on top of a head full of grease. His hair made my skin crawl the way it stood stiff, touching the surface of his white faux fur.

"This is the greatest muthufuckin' show on earth!" he shouted, pimping around the room. "Lemme see what we workin' wit."

We lined up side by side, supposedly standing at attention. My stance was wack. I figured with a missing tooth, and a tarnished silver pimp cup in his hand, he was a true loser. I was pretty much doing it on purpose, until Cinnamon hunched my arm.

"He got big money," she whispered. "And he real quick too."

My eyes lit up like a light bulb. I prayed my tight black halter shirt was appealing enough as he got closer to me. He stopped at each girl, like a Sergeant in the military questioning each of us. He touched, prodded, and did whatever he wanted, to help him make his decision.

"What yo name is?" he asked School Teacher's sister.

"Bambi," she answered meekly.

"No, I'm not tryin' to fuck no Disney characters."

He shook his head and kept moving down the line. When he got to me, I instantly knew he was a boob man. He leaned over just a bit and sniffed my cleavage. Never said a word.

"Mmmmph, mmmmph, mmmmph," the Don Juan look a like said, eyeing me in the face. "Oh, this is it," he said, in Ms. Dottie's direction. "I want lil' magic," he announced. "That's my final answer," he added, with confidence.

Who the fuck is lil magic? I wondered.

When I realized he was pulling on my arm, I hopped out of line. "Why did you call me lil' magic?" I finally asked.

"Cause you look like you can make shit dis-a-ppear," he said, hesitating between each syllable. "Mmmmmm, ummmph." He leaned back on his two-inch high clogs before continuing. "Damn, girl…fuck a dime, yous a fifty-cent piece."

Why in the hell did I have to get this clown? I hesitated for a moment, until he flipped his wad, waving about thirty hundreds in my face. I wasn't sure if I was getting them all, but even fifteen would work. I remembered Daddy's words. "You gotta make double." Then I thought about Cinnamon saying he was quick.

"You ready for me, baby?" he asked.

A smile appeared on my face. "Umm, huh," I mumbled, and took him upstairs to my room. *Damn, I hope Cinnamon was right.*

Once inside my room, I dimmed the lights, and made a comfortable spot on the bed for him to lay back and relax. Each pillow was fluffed to perfection, while he stood behind me and watched. I figured I'd give him a lot of foreplay, then he'd be extra quick, and I'd be back downstairs to make more money.

"Lay down for a minute," I told him. "Let's get to know each other a bit."

"Know you…baby, I don't need to get to know you. He the only one who you need to meet," he replied, pointing to his dick.

"What's your name then?" I asked, feeling a lil' uncomfortable. Hands down, I liked the atmosphere where I'd met G. Rock better than this. At least we could mingle a bit, not just come upstairs and start fucking like dogs in heat. I wanted to stay in a mindset that told me this job was temporary, and that I was only dating these Johns.

By now, I figured Mr. Pimp wasn't gonna tell me his name. He started acting weird by circling my body. The more he walked in circles, the dizzier I became. It could've been the multi-colored shirt he'd just taken off and thrown across my bed.

I took his lead, and starting taking my shirt off too. But he stopped me in the process. "Start from the bottom," he said.

My movements were slow as I removed my pants, one leg at a time. Once again, Mr. Pimp circled me. This time, he stopped and locked his eyes on my ass. I looked over my shoulder to check his focus. Instantly, he dropped his pants down to his knees. No underwear…no boxers…nothing was in sight. Standing there ass-naked was a pitiful situation. I just stared in a daze with my lip hanging, and mouth wide open. I was helping him out by giving him two inches.

"Do you like italain sausages?" he asked, pulling on his tiny dick.

Honey, that's more like a Vienna Sausage, I thought.

"Simon says, bend over and touch your muthafuckin' toes," he commanded.

I obeyed immediately, which made my butt cheeks spread. I knew I had a fat ass. I'd gotten it from my mama. But I felt so stupid bending over in the middle of the floor.

Then from between my legs, I saw him headed my way with his little dick in hand. I had to think quick.

"Condoms are in the drawer!" I yelled.

However, Mr. Pimp was prepared. With the condom already in his hand, he slipped it on with ease, and smiled. *Nigga, if you're not wearing a Magnum I wouldn't be smiling,* I thought. I prepared myself for whatever was about to happen next, and before long, Mr. Pimp was grinding on my ass like he was really doing something. I wanted to laugh, but didn't want to ruin my chances of making money. Besides, I wanted to make Daddy proud.

After finally getting hard, he stuck his baby-sized dick inside my pussy, and began to move back and forth. However, thirty seconds later, he made a few more thrusts, then let out a big sigh. Thank goodness I wasn't in this for the joy, 'cause there was none. He wasn't even a two minute man.

"Wow, yous the shit, lil magic," he said, pulling his pants back up. "I'm comin' back for sure, and I'm gonna make sure I pick you from now on."

"You do that, baby. I enjoyed it," I lied.

"Yeah, I know. I'm surprised the girls didn't tell you how I be tearing they pussy up."

Dude, you can't be serious. A five-year old probably has a bigger dick than you. "Yeah, you did your thing, tiger."

Before long, Mr. Pimp had paid Ms. Dottie my $3,000 fee, and I was back downstairs on the sofa waiting for round two. As I sat there, I couldn't help but smile. With Daddy on my side, I knew my life would slowly get back on track. I liked being on top. It was where I belonged.

Daddy's House

Chapter Thirteen

Three days later, my attitude had completely changed, and I found myself in a state of depression. For days, I'd been sending Tracey MySpace messages, and surprisingly, she never responded. She wouldn't even answer the phone. I figured she'd found out some deep information about my mother, and didn't want to have anything else to do with me. When I made my way into the living room, Sushi, Cinnamon, Luscious and School Teacher were laid out on the plush sofas in relax mode. It was a chill day for most of us; a day full of pampering, getting our hair and toes done, or whatever grooming we needed. Tonight was a big night in the house, so we all needed to look scrumptious.

As soon as I plopped down on the couch, Sushi shoved a drink directly in my face. I wasn't sure what was in the martini shaped glass, but it didn't matter. My nerves were bad, real bad. So, I sipped my drink, hoping to get blasted...needed to be blasted. All of a sudden, I noticed the sofas had been pushed all the way back to the walls.

A few caterers and musicians were starting to file into the house, even though showtime was nearly five hours away. They brought in casseroles, fruit, caviar and expensive cheese platters. The aroma smelled great, and this seemed to be more of a big to-do than the other night.

"Why does it seem like they're overdoing it for this event?" I asked innocently.

"Chica, they are overdoing it," School Teacher said, as she bit into an apple. "Tonight is real important, because the men who are coming are the only ones who have the real potential to shut this place down."

"Yeah, gurl…Senators, Congressman, and all the major political players are coming tonight," Cinnamon revealed. "That's why I gotta make sure my nurses outfit has been pressed and cleaned. I called over to the cleaners five times already. It better be here by five."

She looked a little nervous. Hell, they all seemed a little nervous, except Luscious. She was the mute of the house. Never really heard her say two words. I looked at her, like I wanted to hear what she had to say, but she just turned away and starting filing her nails.

"Yeah, Daddy make us dress in costumes for tonight. I not know what I be. Everybody have gimmick," Sushi said, looking at me strangely. "Who you be, Candy?"

Damn, I wanted to enroll Sushi into some English classes as soon as possible. I smiled a big smile. "Maybe I'll be a secretary. They probably fantasize about getting with their secretaries anyway."

"Oh no, homegurllllll. That's my gig," Cinnanom blurted out. "My gear is already set."

"Um…Um…," Ms. Dottie sounded off, as she cleared her throat. Her interruption startled us all. "Candy," she called off, reading from her clipboard. Surprisingly, I didn't even get eye contact. "Your hair appointment is next, ten minutes top. So, finish vacationing, and be ready," she added sarcastically.

Thankfully, she turned to walk away, 'cause her attitude sucked. Just my luck, she stopped, looked over her shoulder, and added, "Daddy wants you in ponytails. You got Senator Marion tonight. Your clothes have been selected, and are on your bed. Oh, and tell Claude not to forget the ribbons for your hair."

When she left the room, she left me feeling funny. She'd played me in front of everyone.

"Whoa! What did you do to her?" Cinnamon questioned.

I stared off into space. Ms. Dottie was always tough with all of us, but there was something wicked about the way she looked at that moment. Maybe Daddy had told her about my advances toward him. Maybe she was upset because Cat got fired, evicted, or whatever they wanted to call her dismissal. She probably thought it was entirely my fault, and wondered why I was still in the house.

Deep down inside she's gotta know Daddy wants me. He may have turned me down, but only for a season. In my mind, I knew I had to make Daddy mine to survive. He was the only one who could protect me from Big V. The first thing I would do when I got Daddy, would be to fire Ms. Dottie. Who cared that she ran the place for him? All ships eventually get new captains. I smiled at my malicious thoughts.

"You hear me, Candy?" Cinnamon asked again.

"Yeah, I hear you. I didn't do a thing." I shrugged my shoulders.

"She gave you the pervert." They all laughed.

"Who?" I knew something was wrong from the worried expressions on their faces.

"Senator Marion. He likes young girls in real life. Thirteen and below. I guess that's the reason for the pony-tail hairstyle." Cinnamon twitched her lips, as if to say good luck, then she said something that made me want to shit on myself. "Lisa was the only girl we had here under seventeen, so she was his last."

I immediately got chill bumps. "Lisa? What happened with her anyway?"

I could tell it was a touchy subject for everyone by the way they looked at one another. "Well, we were instructed not to talk about it with outsiders, but I guess you're family," School Teacher said. She looked around, making sure the coast was clear before she continued. "About seven months ago, Senator Marion was here, and had his third outing with Lisa. He claimed he loved her, and was taking her away. He needed some secret information on Daddy to be able to blackmail him. Lisa told him everything she knew and started a big feud. Marion tried to even shut the house down. It got ugly, but Daddy worked the situation out. Lisa just never came back. She left one day with one of our bodyguards, and nobody has seen her since. We don't know if she went with Marion, or just disappeared."

"Spooky," I said, before folding my arms. I thought about my upcoming night with Marion. I wasn't looking forward to it, but what could I do?

"Just be careful," Sushi said, rubbing my shoulders. "I got back."

"It's, I got your back," Cinnamon corrected. We all laughed.

"It won't be that bad," Sushi said, moving closer to me. Too close. She was always too close. "What's the wildest thing you done?" she questioned. "Sexually."

I laughed and thought back to Rich. "Probably the time when me and my boyfriend made love inside a haunted house at an amusement park. We had it all planned out. We hopped out the ride once we got inside, and got naked behind one of the waxed mannequins. I made sure not to wear any panties underneath my mini for easy access. We hit us a quicky, while the other cars filled with people kept coming. Then we walked through the doors as if nothing ever happened. That was a thrill. I really wanted us to get caught."

Sushi snickered, making fun of me. "Oooh…me so horny," she said, massaging herself. "Me love long time."

Nobody understood. We were amazed by her.

"Me wildest, nastiest time was when…"

"When what?" School Teacher asked, really wanting to know.

"Me fuck dog."

"You fucked a dog?" Cinnamon asked, jumping up from the sofa. We all followed. Sushi was cool, but she was nasty. Real nasty.

"I gotta go get my hair done," I announced, leaving the room. "Sushi, you need help," I suggested, and laughed all the way to the salon. *Now I know her nasty-ass needs to stop touching me.*

Daddy's House

Chapter Fourteen

An hour later, I walked into my room to a huge surprise. The candy filled room smelled delicious, and I took a deep breath as the chocolate, strawberry, lemon, and other scents cluttered my nose. I walked slowly, wondering if all the other girls had room makeovers, props and treats in their rooms too. I doubted it. Besides, I was the top girl.

My eyes darted to my bed filled with assorted hard candies wrapped in strange shapes and packages. Then, from the corner of my eye, I noticed the vanilla covered strawberries, and fine chocolates that lay on top of the dresser. I moved in that direction, stepping on jolly ranchers and hot tamales that covered the floor.

My walk came to a halt as a glimpse of my image was caught in the mirror. With a part straight down the middle of my head, my long tresses, dangling on each side, swept past my shoulders. The beautifully wrapped bows reminded me of an innocent eight year old on Easter Sunday morning. When I noticed my chosen outfit for that night hanging to my left, I thought this is going too far. The pink, satin ruffled shorts seemed to be a size zero. I shook my head at the thought. There was no way my voluptuous ass was getting in those. The baby doll t-shirt was the only part that made me content. The t-shirt read, *Daddy's* in small print, which gave me an instant smile.

I wasn't sure what the night had in store for me, but anxiety had me at its best. I needed a few sleeping pills to take all of this in. I thought about the meds I'd gotten from School Teacher the other day, and headed for my purse at the top of the closet. However, when I reached inside, I immediately noticed a pack of condoms laying on top of my new sunglasses, along with some edible underwear. I couldn't believe my eyes. The vanilla flavored condoms and freaky underwear stood out like a sore thumb. Ms. Dottie had gone overboard this time. I'd purposefully kept my purse at the top of the closet, to keep anyone from ever going inside. This invasion was past trespassing. It was a violation.

My patience was beginning to run thin. I knew I had to calm myself down before I made a decision that would get me fired. So, after locating the pills, I threw the panties on the dresser, and downed about 800 milligrams. I didn't care if I woke up in time for the party or not. With only a few hours remaining, I crashed on top of the assorted candies and fell asleep.

Two hours later, I stood in front of my mirror, piling dark bronze foundation on my cheeks. Pink accents were the chosen color for the occasion. The eye shadow wasn't my favorite, but it was all I'd been supplied with. I turned my head quickly when my bedroom door opened. It had been locked, so someone had to let the stranger in. My eyes searched for a weapon, but I didn't move. My body continued to stand stiffly, as the short, white man moved toward me cautiously.

"You act as if you weren't expecting me," he said, taking a puff from his funky cigar.

I suspected he could've been my date, but the clock to my right read 10:00 p.m. The party wasn't supposed to start until 11 o'clock, so I thought. My gaze narrowed, and my eyebrows creased with suspicion, before I made my move. He was coming too close and hadn't officially made his business clear.

"I'm Senator Marion Hatchett," he finally said, continuing to move closer.

A little relieved, I let my guard down a bit, but continued to watch him doubtfully. With every move he made, I studied him closer. His pale, somewhat skeletal body, made me nervous. His eyes were bloodshot red, and the cigar that graced his bony hands, limped feebly over his fingers.

I coughed, letting him know the cigar smoke wasn't cool with me. But he continued to puff, and blew thick clouds of smoke my way. His big blue eyes startled me as well, as his stare was frozen, stuck on me. I refused to let my annoyance show. I knew how much the night meant to Daddy. After all, I'd be the first lady soon.

I could tell the Senator was keyed up about the many candies around the room, but seemed to be extra excited about the four inch round multicolored lollipops. He grabbed one of the lollipops by its long stick, and walked around in complete confidence, feeling real comfortable, like he owned the place.

"Ahhhh…," he mumbled. "You look so sweet," he

said, eyeing my pink ruffled shorts that kept creeping up the crack of my ass.

When he spoke, it was as if we'd known each other in a family sort of way. It was weird, because it was almost like he was preparing to molest his own daughter. I couldn't get over the fact that his frame was extremely small for a man. He looked to be in his early fifties, but the girls had already told me he was thirty-eight. All of a sudden, Marion was so close to me, I could count the freckles on his face...twelve in all.

"Candy, sweet Candy," he said, lifting my chin to examine my body. I was half expecting to see him pull out a pacifier for me to suck. "Your age?" he questioned.

I swallowed hard, noticing my throat was extra dry. "Sixteen," I responded, while grabbing my neck, wishing I wasn't in this horror movie. For some reason, I felt bad about telling the lie, even though I'd already been told that he only liked really young girls. His voice wasn't scary at all, it was actually extremely light for a man...almost a soprano tone. But his mannerisms made me concerned. His plastic grin was more than devilish, it was deranged.

For some reason, my hair was extra bouncy, and my ponytails bounced from side to side, so hopefully he believed my age. Whatever products Claude used made me feel like a white chick from a Pantene commercial.

Out of the blue, Marion grabbed my left hand and took a long sniff. "Aren't you sweet...delectable," he whispered, in a softer voice. He ran his nose down to my toes. Kneeling low to the floor, he smashed his cigar into the carpet, designing a deep black hole. I opened my mouth wide. I knew Daddy would have a problem with that or even worse, Ms. Dottie. *That's probably gonna cost me about $200.00 in fines. I'm gonna make you pay for that shit.*

I held my composure as my weird employer for the night massaged each of my toes. Gently he pressed, pulling them frontward then backwards several times. Then he placed his palm flat on the top of my toes, curling them to the floor. My skin cringed with every penetration, as he moaned in delight. Something forced me to take a peek at this freak. Oh hell no. That crazy bastard wore a damn Dora the Explorer watch. That made it official, I had a true nut case on my hands.

After minutes of having my feet examined, massaged, and toes cracked, the novelty had finally worn off. "Ahhh...feet, my most important fetish," he purred, rising to his feet.

The Senator moved away, just as I reached toward the dresser for my candy adorned necklace. I knew I needed something freaky and different to turn this psychopath on. He nodded his dislike, so I stood in place, wondering what he wanted. His eyes begged for something. I just wasn't sure what it was.

For the first time since he'd been in the room, Marion turned his back on me. He walked over to the bed, removed his Bruno Magli shoes, and laid back on the bed. "Come," he instructed, his finger motioning me over.

I moved slowly, as he moaned like something from a horror film. "Myyyyyyy feet, my beautiful feet, the ultimate fetish." His voice was now whinier than before, almost girlie like.

I thought, *damn, he wanna play with my feet again?* When I approached the bed, I wasted no time. I flung my foot up on the bed, ready for my feet and toes to be attacked once again. But Marion shocked me when he whisked my foot away.

"Not yours. Mine," he said. "Suck'em."

My entire face froze for a second, trying to process what he meant. He rested his legs in the air, waiting for my touch. Hesitantly, I reached out, and grabbed his crusty colorless foot. No pigment whatsoever existed.

I shot him a half-ass smile when I noticed him watching me closely. I began slowly massaging my thumb into his arch.

He screamed out a weird scream from below. "Yeahh, baby!"

I hadn't even done anything yet. *This truly is his fetish*, I thought. I rubbed even deeper, putting more motion into my moves. I watched as Marion's eyes rolled back into his head.

"Tongue!" he shouted. "Use your tongue!"

I hated to do it. And prayed I wouldn't throw up. I closed my eyes and did the unthinkable. I licked all around his big toe in a circular motion. The taste was tolerably fresh enough not to send me overboard, but far from mouth-watering. I made myself drift off to dream of a lovely place, blocking out what my mouth was really doing.

Intricately, I gnawed around his father toe, as he made weird slurping sounds on my bed. His back arched, as his body grinded on top of the candy wrappers. Marion was surely reaching his climax!

Surprisingly, he jumped from the bed, and grabbed me by my shoulders. "You look good enough to eat!" he stated.

My mind wondered in a panic. Would he want me to eat him too? He glanced back over to the chocolate covered body scrub, sitting on the dresser, and played a sick kinda footsie. He slid his foot up and down the middle of my thigh, spending extra time around my clit. As I began to moisten, the door slung open wide.

Daddy, dressed in an all cream suit, grabbed me by my waist and pointed my date toward the door.

Without hesitation, Marion yelled, "I paid over $4,000 for this sweet Candy!"

Daddy didn't respond, so Marion shot him a disapproving look, but it didn't matter. Daddy had a hold on me like he'd just broken up a dangerous fight, and was keeping me from my opponent.

After Marion finally left the room, Daddy released me, locked the door, and walked up to me in anticipation.

I just stood there with my arms clenched to my sides. I was both surprised and pleased by his presence. His tongue hung about an inch from his mouth, completing multiple laps outside the perimeter of his lips. My heart told me I wasn't in trouble.

Finally, Daddy made his move. He undressed me with his eyes for several more seconds, before he took possession of my body, pulling me close to his. He looked into my eyes like he was in a daze, sorta mesmerized by my beauty. After taking my arm into his, together we danced, but there was no music.

His silence was turning me on, so I stopped our relaxed dance, as his back brushed against the bed. I pushed at him, trying to get him to lay down, but his weight was too much.

"Lay back," I said, in a firm voice.

Like clockwork, he laid directly onto his back, and I straddled him like I was in charge. He was pleasantly surprised at my aggression.

"I thought you were shy," he said, in shock.

"This is my shy side." I smiled.

I undressed him swiftly, while he lay on the bed. We laughed at the fact that he had to lift up several times to assist me with the task. He was a big boy, and hard to lift; and stark naked, his stomach seemed to roll over his middrift. Still, his sexiness had me going.

Although a hefty man, and not muscled at all, his dick was thick and long, which instantly made me happy. When Daddy grabbed me by my torso, ready to undress me, I snatched my shirt above my head quicker than he could blink. I was ready, and didn't have time for unnecessary foreplay.

I pulled my pink shorts to the side, exposing my crotch, and held the fabric in position. My body language told him it was a go.

He lifted me by my hips easily, pulled off the rest of my clothes and guided me and my pussy where he wanted us to go. He teased momentarily, allowing his curvaceous monster to stroke my clit. It drove me crazy. So crazy my wetness made me wonder if I'd pissed on myself.

His sudden thrust sent me and him both into a frenzy. The bed rocked and swayed, until I felt the warmth of all of him inside. Daddy's entrance sent me into a long moan.

"Ahhhhhh, you feel soooooooo good, Daddy!" I shouted, so the world would know.

His stiff erection became even stiffer. He pounded...a good pound, not the G. Rock pound. He banged and banged like this was his last piece of pussy ever. Finally, he changed his game up, leaving me in suspense. He began lifting my body up and down on his stiff stick, as if he was lifting one hundred and thirty-two pounds of bar bells. My hips thrust at him rapidly back and forth. It felt so good, I did a Moroccan belly dance all over his rod. My movements were driving him crazy.

"Daddy...why...why...you make me wait sooooooo long."

"I...I...can..."

He couldn't even talk. He huffed more and more the closer he came to his climax.

I started meeting each plunge with a scream. I didn't care who heard me. Daddy was the man, and I knew why they called him Daddy. I had a sweet tooth for him, and it ached.

I hopped off the bed and grabbed the body scrub and smeared it all over him. Together we tossed and turned wrapping ourselves in the scent of deep, rich chocolate. I felt delicious, while *my man* got back inside of me, not to mention, smelled good too.

This time it was a lost cause. The moment he re-entered, the deepness of his thrust had us both howling like two dogs.

"I'm cummmmmmmming!" he shouted, in some incoherent language.

"Yes, Daddy. Yes!" I shouted, still pumping like I didn't want it to end. In between my thrusts, I tried to get every drop. I wondered if this had been my best. The answer smacked me in my face. *Yes!*

An hour later, I found myself still in the same position, lounging on top of Daddy's chest. When I realized he wasn't dead, I asked, "Did the Senator really pay three thousand for me?"

"Yep," he answered, in a drained voice. "Even more for the Candy set up."

"Yeah, I hate the fact that Ms. Dottie came in here to set up the room. She was all in my purse," I added, trying to get the bitch fired.

"I told her to do the Candy thing. It was my fantasy. For me and you," he added, before kissing me on the cheek. "I couldn't bear the thought of another man in here with you, with my fantasy."

"I thought you said you don't fool around with the talent?"

"Normally I don't. I had to feel you out first. Make sure you were worthy of this," he replied pointing to his dick.

I grinned. "How much you make around here anyway?"

"About $40,000 a month," he answered, without hesitation. "Sometimes more."

That was the power of booty. I could always take a man totally out of his character when I wanted to. "So, what do you think about me being the new house lady?" I asked, kissing his chest.

"Oh, so 'cause you think Ms. Dottie went in your purse, you want her job? She was probably just sticking the condoms in there. She told me that's where she put them, when I told her to make sure you used one with that pervert."

"I just don't like the idea. Personal belongings are sacred."

"You hiding something?" he asked, with a serious tone.

My lips instantly clutched his, trying to change the mood. I was messing up a good thing. Besides, I had a lot to hide. We tussled a little before making love two more times. When it was all over, the clock read 4 a.m. Before cuddling in my arms for some well needed sleep, Daddy, slipped a necklace from his pants pocket and laced my neck with what he called his special gift to me.

"You gotta passport?" he asked.

I gave him a wierd expression. "I had one. Just gotta get it renewed."

"Good. I might have to take you with me on a business trip soon."

I smiled, held my platinum diamond encrusted chain tight, and fell asleep with the largest smile possible.

Daddy's House

Chapter Fifteen

I swore I'd never fall in love again, and desperately needed to stick to my guns, but it was hard. Daddy made me feel like I was on top of the world again, and it was a feeling I hadn't felt since Rich. All I ever wanted was to be loved, and with a mother like mine, that never happened. I guess in a way, Daddy reminded me of someone who'd been absent my whole life...my real father. Even though Velma tried to play that role, she never measured up. I needed someone to tell me how pretty I was...to protect me, and now I finally had that. Now, I was finally a daddy's girl.

The next morning, Daddy snuck out of my room as if nothing happened, but told me to my face, I was *his* woman. I wanted the world to know, and still didn't understand why we couldn't start with the bitches in *his* house.

I rushed downstairs into the showroom, wanting to show off my chain. The vibe all around me instantly portrayed...HATERS. Realizing my presence was starting to get me different treatment all ready, I strutted with a little extra twist of the hip, just to get the ladies hot.

Four of the girls were sitting around talking until I entered. Then out of the blue, their mouths zipped up tight once I took a seat. When I threw my body across the long chaise, their facial expressions changed completely, and they didn't seem to be interested in whatever program they were initially watching on the tube. I thought, *I'll be getting a cut of their money in no time.*

When I looked at Sushi, my temperament changed. She was staring at the television with glassy eyes. Her sudden outburst made me look too. My eyes followed Sushi's finger which led me to the screen. Tracey's apartment building flashed before my eyes. The news reporter's voice was the same voice that had been telling a horrible story for the last two minutes. I just hadn't been listening.

In a panic, I threw my hands up to my mouth as the tears strolled down my face. I tried to focus on the distorted sounds that came through my ears, but nothing made sense. It couldn't be true. The words *victim, Tracey Holmes,* appeared on the screen. When the cameraman switched positions, and showed a stretcher carrying Tracey's body outside, covered by a white sheet, I flipped. My howl was like that of a mother bear that lost her cub.

"She was all I had!" I screamed in agony. Snot invaded my nose and the upper part of my lip at the same time. Sushi didn't care though.

She attacked me with a bear hug. "No look," she said, trying to cover my eyes. "T.V...no good," she added in a softened tone, as she rocked me back and forth. For the first time, I wanted her closeness. I needed somebody to hug.

"That's right, experts on site believe the body has been here for about four days now," I heard the reporter say. I screamed again, this time uncontrollably.

Cinnamon came running with a box of tissues, while her eyes welled up too. It was so emotional for us all. Several of the girls had now gathered around, and Sushi backed off a bit. Even though my head hung low, and tears kept me from seeing clearly, I used my peripheral vision to scan the room. Oddly, School Teacher and her twin sister were staring me down. I turned in another direction to break away from their gaze, but Luscious was staring too. For some reason, Luscious' gaze went straight to my necklace. I knew she wasn't the jealous type, because she stayed clear from us most of the time, barely ever saying a word.

I clutched the necklace, wondering why all eyes were on me, especially my necklace at a time like this. "Tracey's dead!" I shouted. Then sobbed even more.

This time they didn't dive in with embraces.

"They said it was murder," Ms. Dottie said somberly, making her presence known in the room.

School Teacher moved aside, allowing me to get a good view of Ms. Dottie. She stared at the television with an evil smirk.

"Huh, everybody got a date with the coroner some day."

I jumped up ready to fight. "My cousin may have been slutty, but God bless the dead, she was all I had." My shoulders reared back, and all I needed was for her to make the first move. "House Lady," I spat, as if I was dis-respectin' her position.

My eyes were still watery, but the tears on my face dried without delay. Ms. Dottie was obviously challenging me. Her finger was extended in my direction, like she was about to preach a sermon. "You disrespectful little bitch," she snapped. "You got the nerve to have on Lisa's chain. And you wearing it like it's yours!"

I looked down at my chain, gripping it hard, like she wanted to steal it. Then my neck did a fast swivel around the room. Everyone knew but me. I was so ashamed. *How could Daddy do this to me*, I thought. Lisa was the missing girl, or dead girl as some around here would say. I wondered why Daddy would've given her a chain. Then I thought about my special moment with him. Maybe he wasn't exclusive maybe it wasn't his first time getting down with the talent. And just think, I thought my night with him was priceless.

At the thought of his name, I rushed out of the room, and ran up the steps like a crazy woman. I burst through my door to grab the number Daddy had given me that morning. He told me to use it when I felt like I needed to hear his voice. I crumbled the small white piece of paper between my thumbs, and hurried back down to use the phone. I didn't care who was up for phone time. I was gonna get my time now. As I punched the keys with force, tears fell from my eyes again thinking about Tracey. I wanted to call one of my family members living in Harlem to see if it was official, but I was too afraid. My mind started going crazy. I instantly analyzed an important fact. Big V was released from prison, and now Tracey was dead!

"Hello…hello," a woman kept repeating.

I looked down at the digital phone to get a good look at the number I'd dialed. I quickly matched it up with the number on the paper. "Umm…Ummm, I was looking for Daddy," I said hesitantly, in between my sniffles.

"Well, you've called the right place," the woman sassi-
ly said. "What can we help you with?"

We, I thought. That fat muthufucka played me, was all
I could think.

"Why don't you call back when you can figure out
what you want," she said, before slamming the phone
down in my ear.

I was devastated. I just slammed my head down onto
the desk and cried even more. "Agent Barnes," I finally
said beneath my breath. "I gotta call him." I knew his last
number by heart and prayed it would work. Emotionally, I
didn't know if I was ready to talk to him, but it was worth
a try. I picked up the phone and dialed.

When his answering service picked up, I whined into
the phone, "Agent Barnes, this is Candice..."

Daddy's House

Chapter Sixteen

"Where's that sheet?" Luke whispered.

I watched him scramble through his kitchen drawers. After giving him some pussy, this nigga better not had been lying.

"I thought your shit was straight?" I strolled over to give him a little help. "Move nigga." I yanked the rest of the drawers out, dumping everything on the floor. "Get the hell down there and find that shit." I gazed at his half naked-ass as he went through every piece of paper. I should'a known that any nigga who fucked with Tracey had to be a damn idiot. His ass searched through coupons, old prescriptions and some other bullshit.

"I know it's here, Velma, 'cause I checked for it, and it was here earlier."

"Why would your dumb-ass put it wit' all that shit in that sloppy ass junk drawer anyway?" I yelled. He shot me a goofy Poindexter look. Luke was the funniest lookin' clown I'd seen in years. I should'a known better than to take his ass any further than Vicky's front door. That was the day everybody came to pay their respects and shit before Tracey's funeral.

I showed up over my sista's house sobbin' and shit

actin' like I hadn't killed Tracey wit' the same knife she'd pulled on me. I actually cried the moment her life disappeared from her body that night. First time I'd shed a tear in over ten years.

"Check this, I'ma go in this here bathroom to wash my ass, and when I return, that shit better pop up!" I walked slowly, waiting to see how long it would take for his ass to respond. Silence. I turned back. *What the fuck, I thought I'd schooled this nigga right.* "Luke! Did you hear what I said?"

"Yeah," he whimpered, like a little bitch.

"Well then speak, nigga."

"Uh huh, I hear you. I gotchu."

I swayed my fat ass through his narrow hallway. I felt all claustrophobic and shit. I flicked on the light when I reached the bathroom, and was blinded by bright-ass color. This nigga had yellow walls with big ass pink polka dots spread throughout. *What the hell?* I slammed down the toilet seat to take a shit. I fell deep into thought as to how I was going to get this little bitch. *Was she really ever blood to me?* I strained to let one out. After that one dropped, I was on a roll. Just when the gettin' was good, that crazy mufucka started banging hysterically on the door.

"What Luke, damn, I'm mindin' my damn bizness. What, you wanna see me wipe my ass too?"

"I found it! I found the number to where Candice is at. I told you I would come through."

I could hear his ass jumping around like a damn kid in a toy store. "A'ight, nigga, pipe the hell down. I'll be out in a sec." He turned the knob, trying to come in. "I locked the shit! Now go sit your ass down somewhere, shit!"

"I'll be waiting for round two, baby. Hurry up!"

He repulsed the hell out of me. I don't know what the hell I was thinkin'. Fuckin' my niece's leftover's just for some damn information was more than my insides could stand. The more I thought about it, that shit, was nasty as hell.

When I first saw his ass standing on the curb of my sister's house, wearing a damn orange velour sweatsuit, that should'a been all the signs I needed. If I didn't think he would come through for me concerning this whole Candice ordeal, his ass would'a been dismissed.

He tried to pull some ol', 'we reached for the same biscuit' love shit. So he configured in his retarded ass mind that we must've been destined. I knew from that point, with a little pussy he would be puddy in my hands. So I rubbed past him between a small space to give him *a sample*. His dick got hard instantly. I didn't give a shit who saw it in the fam. I had my mind set on one thing…getting Candice's ass. Now that I got my info from Luke, there was no need for me to go to Tracey's funeral.

After gettin' off the toilet, I stood in front of the sink to take a quick hoe bath. The pink polka dots kept fuckin' with my head. I hit high as possible, low as possible and impossible. The prostitutes in the pen taught me that shit. Hit the face, under the arms and the ass and you done. Time to look for your next conquest.

I slipped into my jeans and a cream sweater and went back to glow worm. That was my name for him. Damn, his ass was bright! *I hope he take the five g's I give him and head straight for the islands. He needs to let the sun kiss all over his ass.*

I reached his tiny hollow kitchen to find his ass scrambling eggs. "Especially for you, baby," he said.

"Yo, how many times I gotta tell you're a…"

"I know, I know, but you so luscious." I stuck out my hand. He knew exactly what I wanted. Luke reached over to the counter and handed me the torn piece of paper. I held it slightly away from my face, and kissed the phone number. I tucked it in my bra, prepared to go forth with my plan. *The shit is on now!*

"You happy now," Luke said.

"I'm 70 percent there. Just chill, you'll get your cash, you hungry bastard."

"Why you gotta talk like that? You too beautiful to act like that." He was serious about this relationship shit.

"Slap some damn eggs on my plate."

"Not until you give me some more ass. I told you I'd be ready for round two. Nobody told you to wash your ass. I gave you what you want, now give me what I want." He smiled, showing that big-ass gap between his two front teeth. I don't know what was wrong with niggas. The more you gave 'em, the more they wanted. I grabbed his ass and pulled him toward the living room, 'cause I knew he wasn't gonna be right until I dropped that sweetness on him.

My big fat ass was spread eagle on his little-ass couch within seconds.

"Turn over so I can go deep," he said.

"Damn, nigga, I'm scrapin' my damn knee. Throw this low-ass, raggedy-ass couch out!" He got lost in my shit before I could get in position.

"It's good," his skinny-ass screeched.

My bloated cheeks could easily swallow his little ass if I let 'em! I couldn't help but laugh at him. *The shit I did for information.* "Hurry up so I can wash my ass again." He let it all out. This time with an attitude.

"I'm tired of you being the damn man in this relationship," he said, with an attitude.

"Relationship? What relationship? Shit, this is bizness, not pleasure!" I hurt his feelings. "Come here, Luke, baby, it's cool. You know how I do." I let him nurse on my pussy. *Niggas are weak for that juicy shit.* I pushed him from between my legs. "That's enough. Damn, save some for later." I hopped off the couch, and went straight to the kitchen. I was hungry. He pulled me back.

"Lay with me a minute. Why you always jumpin' up?" he asked.

"For the third time, this ain't no love connection, nigga, this is bizness!"

"Come on," Luke whined.

I laid there against my will. I didn't do pillow talk with the poor and desperate. His ass wanted to start reminiscing about Tracey. But I could care less about his thoughts or Tracey. I had already got what I needed.

Daddy's House

Chapter Seventeen

When Daddy pushed his big frame through the door, you would've thought he was coming to a funeral the way everybody moped around the house. Every girl seemed to be in a shitty mood, and no money was being made, except for Luscious, who had some broke thug in her room.

I sat at the bar with the same white robe I'd put on after my shower that morning. At six in the evening, we were all supposed to be dolled up and ready for action. Ms. Dottie said we were behind on our quota, but the moral was dead. Sushi had even put on a black, long gown in honor of Tracey, and passed a bottle of Remy Martin VSOP around the room.

Instead, I was on my third glass on Jack Daniels, combined with my forth Prozac, compliments of School Teacher. She had broken down earlier, spilling her guts about how she wanted to leave, but Daddy wouldn't allow it. She said she'd been to the hospital many times on suicide watch, and all she had to show for it was the bottle of pills that now lay smothered in my hands.

I watched Daddy from the corner of my eye stand near the foyer with Ms. Dottie. She was spilling her guts about me, I'm sure. Her eyes kept darting over to the bar, hoping to get some type of reaction out of me, but it wasn't working. She didn't even give him a chance to take off the designer scarf, nor the black leather jacket he wore.

The more she whispered, the louder my roommates became. I couldn't hear a thing. Finally, Ms. Dottie turned on her heels with an attitude like she was fed-up. Daddy, on the other hand, took off his coat, slung it over his arm, and pimped my way.

As soon as he was within three feet of me, I jumped up and started yelling like we'd been married for years. My hair was uncombed, attracted all kinds of static, and spread over my head.

"Who the fuck was the woman who answered your phone, huh?" I badgered. "You told me I was your woman. Didn't you?" My head bounced up and down, like I had the power.

Daddy moved closer to me, unmoved by my craziness. His huge arms stretched toward my shoulders, in an attempt to calm me down. "Candy, listen to me. We need to talk. But you gotta calm down," he said, in a more authoritative tone.

He looked around at the girls, and even the extra workers who'd just arrived at the house. "I want this room empty," he said calmly. The fire in his voice was brutal enough to send the police scattering. "And every working piece of ass better be dressed in their finest attire in less than one hour!" Everyone scattered like roaches.

Daddy grabbed me by the waist lightly, and led me to a small table off to the side of the showroom. "Sit down," he said, helping me sit. "First of all, I'm sorry to hear about your cousin. Ms. Dottie told me everything.

Secondly, what's this other woman bullshit?"

He took a seat across from me, but decided to pull his chair closer. I couldn't believe he could still act so cool while he lied flawlessly.

I gazed into his eyes, wanting to smack the shit outta him. But he was three times my size. "I called the number you gave me, and a woman answered," I said matter of factly. "You can't change that," I added, as he tried to interrupt me. I had the palm of my hand held toward his face, which told him to stop lying.

He grabbed my hand gently, then squeezed harder and harder. He leaned over the table into my face, while speaking with the deepest anger I'd seen. My circulation was almost completely shut off.

"If you don't calm the fuck down, you're gonna regret it!"

Chills ran through my body. I'd never see him like that before. Now, I understood all the rumors around the house about how he could get.

"Now, if you called the number, little girllllll, then you spoke to the woman who answers my calls. All, I repeat…all my calls go to her, because that's my answering service. Shelly is my operator's name. You'll get to meet her one day."

I looked at him, wondering if he was telling the truth. Then I thought back to the other day when I called him. The woman kept saying we, she just never presented the situation clearly.

Feeling like I was in the wrong, I hopped up, jumped into his lap, wanting to mourn with him about Tracey. I hadn't slept all night, and would've given anything for him to come up to my room just to console me. Daddy

looked away from me as I held him tightly. He seemed a
bit standoffish.

"What's wrong?" I finally asked.

"I got a little beef with you."

"What?" I wiped away the tears with the palm of my
hands that had just begun to fall.

"I asked you before if you had anything to hide. I'll
ask again...do you?"

Damn, what does he know? I stretched my neck back
like he had offended me. "Heck no. Why you say that." I
stuck my hand into the pocket of my robe nervously, in
search of some more tissue. Just then, I felt the hardness
of Lisa's necklace rub against my hand.

"Explain the two I.D.'s in your purse, Ms. Danielle
Crouch." Daddy's words resonated inside my head. *How
did he know?*

"You been snooping in my things?" I snapped, trying
to bide myself some time. I yanked the necklace from my
pocket and slammed it face down on the wooden table.

"Who is Danielle Crouch?" he demanded.

He pushed me off of him with force and stood up,
only to tower over me. I was afraid, but knew how to
coax my way out of hostile situations. I'd been in plenty
before.

"My abusive boyfriend, who I told you about, had me
so scared I didn't know what to do." I stopped in mid-
sentence, just to throw in a few extra sniffs. "I got that
fake I.D. made in the name Danielle Crouch to get an
apartment and phone. I was too scared to use my real
name, because I knew he could find me."

Daddy nodded. He really wanted to believe me. He'd
already made it clear when I first met him that he didn't

trust females.

"That's it, I swear."

By now my face was flushed, damn near purple. I studied Daddy for a moment, to see if he was falling for it. He studied me for a few moments, cupped his chin, made a contemplating humming sound, then reared back in his seat.

"So what about this necklace you gave me?" I fired.

"What about it?"

His nonchalant tone pissed me off. "Oh, so that's how we playing it? I'm the only one who can be honest?"

"I'll tell you what. Go upstairs, pack a bag, and I'll tell you about it on our way out of town."

My smile was so big, I could've been hired as a clown. "Out of town?" I questioned.

"Yes…unless you have something else to do. I mean, I assume Tracey's funeral won't be for another four to five days. You'll be back by then," he added.

I had no intention on going to the funeral, but at least he reminded me that I needed to pretend like I was going. Besides, going out of town might've been the best thing for me now. *Even if it is with my cheating new man.*

I marched upstairs with my necklace, Lisa's necklace, *our* necklace in hand. However, the moment we pulled off the property, I wanted answers.

Daddy's House

Chapter Eighteen

If someone had told me a month ago I would be riding in Daddy's brand new black S600 Benz, I would've told them to
kiss my ass. I couldn't believe my life had the possibility of turning out okay. Breaking away from my thoughts, I turned to look over at Daddy through my new $420.00 Chanel sunglasses, compliments of my *new man*. The shades were perfect, and kept him from seeing my eyes. That's what I liked about shades, they seemed to hide the truth.

Daddy's hands gripped the wheel with confidence, like he was some type of millionaire. I just leaned back and watched him drive with a smile; just being in his presence was enough for me. The oversized chinchilla mink he wore was unnecessary for November, but I guess being a show off was his style. We'd just come back from a night on the town at the Mohegan Sun Casino in the eastern part of Connecticut, and I couldn't have been happier.

That night was our first time hanging out. The day before, we stayed inside the room and screwed all night. I was really feeling him, and thought about how our relationship was changing over the last few days. *Love, it had to be*, I thought. Surprisingly, he was falling in love too. He never said it, but when he told me we were gonna stop by his aunt's house in the Bronx on the way back, I knew I had him hooked. Hell, what else could it have been if he wanted me to meet his family this soon?

I actually wanted to meet his people too, but was a little nervous. Surely his family were like any other dysfunctional bunch in America; filled with dope feigns, thieves, talkative aunts, and worrisome ass nieces and nephews. Still, more days alone with him would've been fine with me. But hell, Thanksgiving was the next day, and at least I wasn't spending it alone.

Being away from the house was a good feeling, almost like an unbelievable fantasy. I looked over at Daddy one last time, noticing him snap his fingers, and nod his head. An old school song by the Whispers flowed through the speakers. *I'm Gonna Make You My Wife*. It was perfect for us. I instantly leaned forward, and turned up the volume. I loved to see him happy.

"I'm gonna buy you some rings," Daddy sang along. "And everywhere you go, everyone will know, that it's real, what you make me feel. I'm gonna make you my wife."

I was only twenty-three, but that old school shit had meaning.

He turned to find me singing the chorus too. "I'm gonna make you my wiiiiife," I hummed.

Damn, that sounded good to my ears, but the valet attendant headed toward my door was getting ready to ruin our moment. As soon as we hit the circular tiled driveway, I knew my special moment was over. My door flew open, and a professional voice greeted me.

"Good evening Miss. Welcome to Kensington's."

I stepped out proudly in the new sleek, black Dolce and Gabanna dress Daddy got me that morning from one of the hotel shops, and smiled from ear to ear.

"You look good, baby girl," Daddy said, coming around to the passenger side to greet me. He shot the valet guy a quick frown. I don't think he wanted anybody enjoying the good looks but him.

I thought I was pretty damn tempting, if I could say so myself. We strutted into the five-star restaurant hand in hand. Once at the table, I thought about asking him why his wandering eye kept looking at the young girl who'd brought us our menus and wine glasses. Then decided against it, since we'd already dismissed the issue about the necklace and my fake I.D. We agreed we'd start fresh, no distrust whatsoever.

"So, you ready to meet the fam tomorrow?" he asked, after the waitress left our table.

I shrugged my shoulders. "Sure, but I would love to stay here a few more days with you. I've had enough turkey to last a lifetime."

"C'mon, baby girl. There's nothing better than family."

I shook my head. "Yeah. Well, for me, family symbolizes distrust."

"For me too." He laughed. "You know how many times my thievin' ass nephews have stolen from me? My sister even called the cops on me before," he said, without a care.

"Nothing seems to bother you. I mean, it's like you have alligator skin or something."

He laughed. "You think so, huh?"

I nodded my response.

"I guess since my mother died, it changed me. I mean, I'm all talked out. Nothing else matters. It's all about business. I mean...until I met you." He grabbed my hand and kissed it.

"I wish I could've met her," I responded, earning myself some brownie points.

"You will."

What the hell are you talking about, I wondered, *he'd just mentioned that she was dead.* "Your mom is..." I decided not to say a word. Maybe the wine had him going.

Daddy laughed, then shook his head up and down. "She is, but that doesn't mean you can't meet her," he responded. "So, where's your mother buried?"

Damn, he caught me off guard. I grabbed my glass and took a sip of water to buy me some time. "Washington Memorial, out in Secaucus, Jersey," I finally answered.

"Oh yeah. Well, we'll go pass there tomorrow on our way to the Bronx. It's just over the George Washington Bridge. I wanna pay my respects since I might officially be in the family soon."

My cheeks turned rosy. I quickly took another sip of water, damn near guzzling the whole glass.

"Besides, we'll visit my mother's grave too. I do it every Thanksgiving. It's not far from your moms," he added, as the waitress appeared to take our order.

I started coughing uncontrollably, and jumped up from my seat, almost pulling the white linen tablecloth along with me.

"Order for me, baby. Anything," I said, in between coughs.

I jetted to the bathroom, and into one of the stalls. As my body slid against the wall, my thoughts went haywire. *Why do I keep allowing myself to get in these crazy situations? At what point am I just gonna be honest with people...with myself?* Daddy was the one person in my life who really seemed to care about me, so I knew it was wrong to start off our relationship this way. *I gotta figure out a way to get out of this shit.*

The next day, I found myself in a laid back position once again; this time not as happy. The ride to Bronx seemed like an eternity, as I thought about stopping by to visit my fake mother's grave. Daddy made it clear that dinner was at 4 p.m. sharp, and we'd make our gravesite visits before dinner.

Even after spending all that time in the bathroom the night before, I still hadn't figured out how to talk my way out of this mess.

I leaned back further in the seat, sniffling every few minutes, trying to spring a fake sickness on Daddy with ease. For the most part he'd been ignoring me. I was beginning to get worried until he said, "You coming down with something?"

I sniffed. "Yeah...I think." I threw my hand up to my forehead to check for a fever.

"Close your eyes and rest," he insisted, squeezing my thigh. "We'll be there within the next hour."

"Okay," I replied, knowing that my eyes would close, but rest would be the furthest thing from my mind. I

turned my body toward the window, keeping my ̤
from his view, and pretended to get some sleep. My ̤
was to sketch out what I would do the moment we hit th̤
cemetery, where he thought my mother was buried. For
minutes, my thoughts switched from a breakdown right in
the car as soon as we pulled up, to maybe a deadly fall on
one of the headstones. Whatever the case may be, Daddy
was no fool, so it would have to be good.

I even took a few minutes to pray. Something I didn't
do often. Unfortunately, my mother didn't do church. But
when I was younger, my grandmother taught me about
the love of God. I knew He was real. I believed. I just
prayed He'd get me through this one, like He did so many
other times. I promised I'd start going to church if He'd
let me off the hook with this one. *For real this time.*

Soon, my moment of truth came. Twenty minutes
later, I saw the huge black iron-gate from the road, and
the thousands of headstones that lay inside. Before we
even turned into the gate, my heart rate sped up a notch. I
wasn't sure if Daddy's mother rested here, or mine. Small
beads of sweat began to form on my forehead, as I continued to work on my academy performance.

When I felt the car make several turns, I knew it was
show-time. "Wake up, baby girl," Daddy said, in a soft
voice.

"Huh." I turned around like I didn't hear what he said
or knew where we were. The scenery was morbid. It was
a dreary day, so the lack of sun, matched my miserable
mood.

"You get some rest?"

"A little," I said, looking at the many people walking
with fresh flowers. "I don't feel so well." I waited for his

reaction before I continued. "I feel a lil' dizzy."

"Which way?" he asked, obviously ignoring my question, as we came to a crossroad in the cemetery. The car came to a complete stop and my heart did the same.

I didn't answer, 'cause I couldn't get my thoughts together fast enough. I knew we rode past thousands of graves, and I never acted like we passed my mother's grave.

"Right or left?" he asked, with a raised voice.

I pointed to the left with one hand, and held my forehead with the other. There was a good chance that he would believe I was sick, 'cause now I was sweating like hell.

"You'll be okay, baby girl. Daddy gon' take care of you."

"No, you don't understand. I don't think I can get out."

"You got to. While you were sleeping, I realized we didn't have enough time to visit both of our mothers graves before dinner, so I decided to come see yours. It's only right that you see your mom on Thanksgiving. So, let's do this." He smiled. "Show me the way."

I didn't have many choices left. We were near the end of the enclosed cemetery, which had a mausoleum in the center. "Right here. Pull right here," I pointed.

Within moments, Daddy pulled on the side of the grass and hopped out, like he was rushing to put out a fire. *What is the big deal? It's supposed to be my mother, not yours.*

The hair on the back of my neck stood up as I looked at the headstones in my view. I wondered what my next move should be. By the time he got around to open my door, I had thrown my head into my hands and made myself cry hysterically.

I thought about throwing up right in the front seat of his plush car, but I wasn't sure if that would even get me off the hook. He seemed so determined. Maybe he knew about me. Maybe this was all a game. Why wasn't I brave enough to just say, "Look, I lied. My mother is alive and well just got out the pen as a matter of fact."

Daddy gently grabbed me by my arm, helping me from my seat. "I know…I know…," he kept repeating.

Together we walked real slow, like he'd just picked me up from the hospital. I'd cry a little bit, and then take a few baby steps forward. This bullshit continued for several minutes. Daddy led me in the direction of a bunch of headstones that seemed old and outdated. I quickly scanned a few names and dates, noticing we'd been in the old rich white section. One of the headstones read 1899-1945 and another 1899-1952. I stopped abruptly.

"This is the wrong way." I cleared my eyes to refocus. "This way," I said, shedding a few more tears.

We turned around, and I took him straight toward the mausoleum. All of a sudden, I felt like someone was watching me. Every time I stopped to look, or turn around, no one was there. A few white couples were nearby paying respects, but they weren't even looking my way. Daddy kept looking down toward the ground, clocking the names on the headstone. He had no idea the move I was about to pull on him.

As soon as we stepped inside the mausoleum, Daddy's facial expression showed he was impressed. "Oh, she had money, huh? Your moms was gettin' it?"

Why the fuck am I even going through all this, I

thought. I nodded as my body shivered. The search had to go quicker. Much quicker before he asked too many questions. I walked ahead of Daddy, looking for the perfect name, a black name. Most sounded like old Irish names, some even Italian. Then it stared me in the face. Elaine Blackwell- 1975-2004.

My body stopped directly in front of the granite stone. "This is it," I said, allowing my fingers to run across the engraved letters. I envisioned my mother's entire body being pushed into the large stoned wall, hoping it would make me cry naturally. It wasn't working.

Daddy moved in closer. Suddenly, I dove my head underneath his shoulder. "I can't do this," I cried. This time my cry was extreme, over the top. Most people would've thought it was the day of the funeral. The few people around us watched as he inched me back to the car.

"This is too much for you, huh?" he asked.

I nodded.

It seemed as though I'd finally gained his sympathy. "I understand. Let's go eat," he said, helping me get back into the car.

As we pulled away, a slight grin crept on my face. I couldn't believe I'd pulled it off. *Yeah, somebody contact the Academy out in California, because I just won best actress*, I thought. However, my joy quickly faded as thoughts of my real mother entered my mind. The more I thought about it, the more I realized she was alive and well. However, if it were up to me, her ass would've been six feet under for real.

Daddy's House

Chapter Nineteen

By the time we pulled up to Daddy's aunt's house, I was emotionally drained. I'd lied twenty-two times, and more tales were surely on the way. When we stepped on the porch, the loud noise told me this was a hood function, so get ready.

"Well, well, well…look what the cat brought in!" a burgundy-headed woman hollered, as soon as we walked through the door. "And who is it this time, playa?" she added, looking directly at me.

"Aunt Jean, how many times do I have to tell you to stop calling me that," Daddy responded.

"Why not? I hope you don't think I'ma call your ass Daddy," she replied, with a slight laugh.

"This is Candy," Daddy said.

I hunched his side, reminding him that we'd agreed Candy was no longer my nickname, and then showed all my teeth to the woman with the bad color job.

"I mean Candice. This my lady, Candice."

"Hey…how are you?" I smiled.

"Uh..huh…whatever you say. Come on in and make yourself at home. I'm glad you came to have dinner with us. We'll be ready to eat in about an hour. Go on in there to the family room and see your Uncle Manny, boy. He been waitin' on you."

I thought, *damn, how was I gonna make it an hour as hungry as I was.* My stomach growled, looking at the old-fashioned table cloth filled with two huge fried turkeys, ribs, barbecued chicken, macaroni and cheese, stuffing, and every green vegetable ever grown from the ground. It looked like everything was already done to me.

Daddy pulled me along, and held me close as we walked into the cluttered family room. It seemed more like a party than a Thanksgiving dinner gathering. People lined the walls with drinks in their hands, talking loud and having a good time. Everyone glared when we walked in, my arm tucked under his.

"Mannnnnnnn, you got a dime piece wit' you this time!" an older man with a scruffy beard shouted.

Daddy just gave his customary nod and I smiled. Then from the corner of my eye, I caught a glimpse of an evil scowl. A tall, slender guy stood behind Daddy, wearing a pair of saggy jeans and a Sean John oversized shirt. He didn't look familiar, but he stared me down liked I owed him money.

"What's up, baby boy?" Daddy shouted, slapping his palm into the young man's hand.

The way the two of them embraced, I knew they were cool.

"Yo, Candy…I mean Candice. This here my nephew, J-Cee."

"Hello," I said, with a smile.

"Yeah," he said, throwing me shade.

I could tell Daddy didn't like how he was treating me, but let it slide. "So, where you been hiding?" Daddy asked.

"Rikers," J-Cee replied.

"Boy, you need to cut that shit out. Three strikes you out. I know this your twelfth time."

I didn't say a word to anyone. They all looked at me strange, especially J-Cee. He couldn't even pay attention to his uncle, 'cause he was clocking me so hard.

"Where I know you from?" J-Cee blurted out.

My response was slow and well thought out. "Not sure."

"You from New York?" he asked.

"Nah," I answered. "From Chi-Town." At least that wasn't a total lie. I did live there for a short time when I first got in the program.

Daddy looked at me. "I thought you were from East Orange, Jersey?"

Shit, I forgot I told him that. "Umm...I'm originally from Chi-Town, but moved to Jersey when I was five." Hopefully he believed me.

J-Cee cut his eyes at me, just about the same time my stomach got hit with sharp pains. As he continued to stare me down, I scanned my memory of previous dates, or even guys I'd met casually over the years. Nothing registered. Then I wondered if we'd ever sold him some coke. *Nah*, I thought. He didn't look like he had enough money to buy weight. *Damn, I hope he just got me mixed up with one of his girls or some shit.*

After listening to Daddy talk shit with his Uncle Manny for a half an hour, his aunt finally called everyone to eat. As I walked to the dining room area, I said a silent prayer, thanking her for not making me wait the whole hour. As hungry as I was, if it had been any longer, I surely would've passed out.

"Are you sure I don't know you from somewhere?" J-Cee asked, as we sat down at the table.

"Nephew, leave my baby alone," Daddy said, before I could respond. "She don't hang around with lil' boys like you."

Yeah, lil' boy leave me the hell alone, I thought, as more of Daddy's family members began to take their seats around the delicious food. The last thing I needed was extra attention. However, I wasn't so lucky, because J-Cee obviously didn't feel the need to take his uncle's advice. All throughout dinner, he stared at me, which made me extremely uncomfortable. However, I made sure to keep Daddy's eyes on me, so he wouldn't notice. The last thing I needed was drama on a beautiful Thanksgiving Day with my new man.

As we were leaving several hours later, J-Cee met us at the door. "Unc, man, we gotta talk. How 'bout makin' some time for me later tonight?"

"I got something important I gotta take care of tonight. Holla at me tomorrow, nephew."

"Man, it's important, so answer when I call."

Daddy looked like he knew something was wrong. "You a'ight?" he asked, with concern.

"Yeah, I'm good. We just gotta talk."

"No doubt. If I get a minute, I'll call tonight," Daddy responded, giving J-Cee a pound.

"Come on, Daddy. I'm tired," I said, trying to get out the door. I prayed that J-Cee's important information wasn't about me.

As we got into the car, I turned my heated seat on and got comfortable. The day had been a long one, but cuddling up with Daddy at his place would make it all better.

Daddy pulled up to the gate just about the same time I woke up from my short nap on the ride from the Bronx. I'd been sleeping all day, every chance I got. I knew I was tired from all the driving we'd done, but all that good Thanksgiving food didn't help either. I prayed the sleepiness was the cause of me thinking I was back at the house. I blinked, hoping it was all a dream. Rising in my seat, my head moved from right to left.

Nervously, I asked, "Why are we here?"

He hesitated before he spoke. The first clue which told me this wasn't good, was that he couldn't even look me in the eye.

"I got some serious business to take care of before I take you to my spot. I gotta make sure it's safe for you first."

"I don't care!" I shouted.

I moved around in my seat, anxiously leaning in closer to Daddy. However, when I did, he went the opposite way. He didn't show much emotion, which was the norm, but I needed him to feel what I was saying.

"I just wanna be with you," I pleaded. "Please don't make me go back in there. You promised."

A couple of seconds later, a light popped on in the foyer. Ms. Dottie was probably waiting patiently to grin in my face. "She knows I'm coming back," I pointed to the house.

He shook his head. No words. Just confirmation.

Daddy seemed cold. I'm not sure if the situation with his mother had gotten to him on the ride back, but my guess was he needed therapy.

"You wanna be with me?" I asked, snatching his hand tightly.

"Of course I do," he said, finally looking at me.

"Tell me you love me."

He said nothing.

"Tell me you love me," I repeated. "I know you do."

"I like you more than any of the others, Can…"

The others? What the fuck? Was he comparing me to the other bitches in the house? Or was he saying his other women? I didn't care. I just wanted to be with him. His other broads could be deleted later. "Can…dice," I finished.

"I got a lot going on. I'll explain later," he said, taking a heavy breath.

This time, he grabbed my hand, and clutched it. His silence told me he was waiting for me to get out. I looked over my shoulder at the house, then back at Daddy. He turned his head swiftly, sure to miss my stare. "Good night," he said.

I opened my car door, thinking, *I saw this shit in a movie once.*

Chapter Twenty

Something in me forced my body to do as I was told. I had no intentions on being back at the house again until I married Daddy and became half owner. Even if Daddy had something to do, why couldn't I chill at his spot? I felt like I was being played, and was starting to question how much he really cared for me.

My presence back in the house didn't feel good at all. When I opened my bedroom door the next morning, Ms. Dottie appeared immediately. Hell, it was only 10 a.m., so I knew she wasn't expecting me to entertain anyone before breakfast. She stood like a statue, keeping me from exiting the room.

"So, what brought you back?" she asked.

I threw her a smirk, like I was confident about my relationship with Daddy. "Oh, it won't be for long. Daddy said just a few days."

"Sure. I've heard that one before."

"Umm...huh." *Her time was getting shorter by the day, she just didn't know it.* "Is there anything else you need from me?" I asked, brushing against her. She knew I wanted to leave my room.

Ms. Dottie bent down to reach into the large white

cardboard box that lay on the floor beside her. When she displayed the clear vase with twelve beautiful red roses, I smiled broadly. *He really does care*, I thought.

I grabbed the vase and rushed downstairs to show off my flowers. The moment I sat them on the table, I looked around for someone to share my moment with me as I reached for the card. Sushi was just coming through the door; the perfect person to spread the word throughout the house.

"Sushi, look what Daddy just sent me."

She tried to smile, but it was fake. Something was definitely wrong. Normally you couldn't keep her ass from smiling. "Are you alright," I asked.

"We talk…okay?"

"Sure." Her choppy English had gotten on my last nerve. I needed a girlfriend from the hood to share my happiness with. "C'mere," I said, pulling her by the arm. I snatched the card off the stem and read.

Tulips are for Mistresses, Roses are for Lovers. I am willing to take this one step further. Hope you're thinking about me the way I'm thinking about you. I'll be back for you real soon, my sweet candy treat.

Senator Marion Hatchett

My mouth remained wide open from the initial shock, but Sushi's response topped mine. With a cold blank stare, I knew we had to talk. Sushi told me Ms. Dottie was in the process of hiring a new girl in the front office, so we needed to sneak to a place where we'd have some privacy.

She kept pointing to the front of the house nervously. "The gym," she finally said, in a low voice.

I thought about throwing the flowers away, but just grabbed the card with Marion's information, and followed Sushi. If I ever needed money, he'd be the man to call. He seemed to be the type that could be jerked easily.

Standing near the stair climber, Sushi and I stood close like two secret lovers. I just knew she was pregnant. That's the only thing I could think of serious enough to have her acting like that. *Oh, no* I wondered. *Daddy's baby?* I'd kill his ass and Sushi too for that matter.

"Spill it," I finally said.

"So much me need to say."

"Just say it," I ordered, with a louder voice.

"Shhhuuush." Sushi seemed to be very afraid. More than before.

"Ms. Dot not like. She trashed you room. Not Cat."

"Are you telling me, Cat didn't do that shit to my room?"

"Yes."

My eyes grew to the size of watermelons as I folded my arms, and paced the floor. The first chance I got, Ms. Dottie had some explaining to do. Then I was gonna kick her ass, and fire her on the spot. Daddy would back me when I explained what happened. I just knew he would.

I was on my fifth circle around the gym, when Sushi said the unthinkable. "Daddy pay me to spy on you."

I wanted to rip her nose ring from her fucking nostril. "What did you say?" I asked, making sure I heard her correctly.

Sushi held her head downward. "Me so shame. He pay me lots."

"Yeah, yeah, yeah. Save it! Spy on me how?" I got up real close in her face.

"He say just watch you. Anything bad tell him. Me like you Candy, really do. You friend. Only friend me got. That's why when Ms. Dot told me to try hang out with you week ago on you day off, I did. No 'cause they paid, but 'cause me wanted to."

"What did you tell'em?" I asked, pushing Sushi against the treadmill. I had to get gangsta with my girl. Using both hands and all my strength, I gripped her by her collar. I had no intentions on hurting Sushi, but she didn't need to know that.

"Nothing...I swear. Me told truth. Just go shopping," she stuttered, "and eat with Tracey. That's all me say."

I rewound the events of dealing with Sushi in my head. I thought about the times when Sushi could've told something about me that would get me in serious trouble. Nothing registered. It was all too crazy.

When my grip loosened off of Sushi's collar, she felt like it was okay to speak again. "Candy..."

"Candice, bitch!"

Her face wrinkled. She didn't know how to take my sudden attitude change. "You betrayed me."

"No...no...no. It's Daddy. He fool you. He fool all the girls."

"This is about me and you." I felt like I still needed to defend my man.

"He do this again...all the time. You get hurt." She started crying- tears flowing like the Nile. "Please, please...stay away from him."

"Stay away from who?" Ms. Dottie asked, standing in the doorway.

Our secret meeting was obviously over, and I had a lot to think about. For starters, I made a mental note to put everyone I'd come in contact with over the past few weeks in two separate categories, *those for me*, and *those against me*.

Daddy's House

Chapter Twenty-One

"What in the hell is going on with you?" I heard Daddy say, as he burst through the front door. The door slammed hard, real hard, almost coming off the hinges. I leaned over the railing at the top of the stairs to eavesdrop a little better.

"What do you mean, what's going on with me? You should ask yourself that," Ms. Dottie responded professionally, but a little louder than normal.

"It's been two days, and you've only serviced two customers. We can't survive like this!" he shouted. "Why haven't you been calling some of our regular clients to let them know we have new talent like you normally do? Money gotta be made if everybody wants to get paid this week, including you!"

"Oh, so now you feeling the heat. You seem to be whisking the girls off whenever you want, firing the others when you want, and lowering the moral...period. I can't do my job under these circumstances. Besides, it's not what we agreed."

Anxiety got the best of me. I made my way down the steps just as Ms. Dottie said 'not what we agreed'. I wondered what they had to agree upon that would have them looking into each other's eyes that way.

"I knew you would come back for me. A man of his word," I said, walking up to Daddy. I shot Ms. Dottie a nasty smirk. The bitch was mad jealous. There was no way she could hide it.

"Let us finish," Daddy shouted my way, just as my arms opened and reached for his neck.

Damn, I can't even get a hug, I thought. And he smelled good as hell too. It had taken two days for Daddy to come get me. But yes, he was right. The house had been unusually slow, but it wasn't our fault. I didn't even like Ms. Dottie, but didn't think she deserved all the slack he was giving her. Maybe it was slow because of the Thanksgiving holiday. Hell, dicks needed holidays too.

I looked at Ms. Dottie thinking about how she'd changed over the last few days. She definitely wasn't putting the full court press on us about our schedules like she normally did, and even forgot to call me down for a customer who was interested in me last night. She'd even turned a few customers away the day before. It was very unlike her.

Daddy shot me a mean look. So, I switched back up the stairs hoping he would take a look at my backside. I wanted him to want me. Instead, he kept chewing Ms. Dottie a new asshole. I rushed to my room, and packed my bags as quickly as possible. I threw my stuff into the two new Gucci duffel bags I'd gotten in Connecticut. What didn't fit, stayed. I figured, leave it for charity. Whoever the new girl was, who'd occupy this room, could have it, compliments of Candy. *Sweeet Candy*. I laughed thinking about Senator Marion.

I glanced around the room momentarily as I prepared

myself to leave. A new chapter in my life would be good. Suddenly, Daddy appeared at the door; his face twisted up like he had a beef to settle.

"Just saying goobye," I said, trying to lighten the mood.

He never smiled.

"Sit down," he ordered. He shut the door, and locked it, then rushed toward me. "You got something to tell me," he asked.

I frowned. "No," I responded hesitantly.

"Well, I went by Tracey's funeral today. Surprisingly, you weren't there."

I could've shit bricks.

"I told Ms. Dottie if you asked to go, allow it. But you never tried. I wonder why?"

He pulled the obituary with a picture of Tracey from his pocket, and tossed it on the bed next to me. Visions of Tracey's face made me cry instantly. The first real tears I'd shed in days.

"Enough of that," he said harshly. "Why weren't you there?" he drilled. Your Aunt Vicki was there. A lot of your family was there."

My heart pounded. I waited for him to say my mother's name. He just looked down at me, while he paced the floor.

"I'll explain it all later. Let's just go," I pleaded.

"Go where? There's money to be made around here. You see my nephew, J-Cee, hipped me to how you ruin lives. How you love money. Well, I love money too."

My heart felt like it fell in the bottom of my stomach. "What are you talking about?"

"He told me about how you ended up going on a run

for your mother once, and ended up sleeping with her Columbian connection. You good at seducing the big men in charge aren't you?"

I wanted to scream nooooooo, and defend myself, but Daddy moved toward me with speed, managing to gain a tight grip on the back of my neck.

He continued like it was a strain to speak. "You fucked the connection, and started getting product from him real cheap." He moved closer to my face, tightening his grip. "How much were you getting? Three, four, kilos, at a time?"

I was too scared to lie. I was too scared to speak.

"You had a good thing going, making a lot of money, and hiding it from your mother. You knew she'd kill you if she found out you betrayed her. Didn't you?" he badgered.

"That's not what happened," I lied.

"Yeah it is. The connec cut your mother off, never dealt with her again, just you. So when your Columbian lover got caught, it was time to snitch, huh? The feds thought it was Big V who had been making all the money from him. But it was you. Sly little whore."

"Daddy, please believe me," I begged.

"This is why I can't get serious about women. And just think…I took you outta here like you were my woman. And look at this bullshit you pulled with your own fam. You'd probably do the same shit to me."

"No, I wouldn't!" I jumped up hoping to plead my case.

"So, I guess in your mind your mother is dead." He shook his head at me with disgust. "You had me go to some white muthufucka's grave, didn't you!" he yelled, then paced the floor again. "I went to that funeral hoping to find your mother. J-Cee knows what she looks like, but she wasn't there. I would'a brought her back here so she could kill you slowly."

I had nothing to say. Shame was all I thought as I held my head low. Then, I thought about how the real Daddy was beginning to surface. The Daddy who would tell me to my face, he would allow someone to kill me.

"How could you allow your own mother to take the weight for you? And your uncles, and other family members? That's the worst betrayal there is," he added. "How long will it take for you to betray me?"

I shook my head back and forth. "I would never betray you." I cried a few tears, even though he made it clear he wasn't interested.

"You thought she wouldn't find out, stupid. That's what the feds do…they turn every defendant involved in a case against one another. They told Big V you snitched on her, then they told the Columbian connec it was you who would testify against him too."

"I never snitched on anybody!" I shouted.

Daddy smiled. "The truth came out…and it all comes back to you," he said, headed toward the door. "Ummmph….ummmph…umph. So fine on the outside, yet so untrue on the inside." His head shook in disgust. "Now gear up!" His voice resonated throughout the room. "While I been away from the house being tricked by your ass, my business is going under. You gotta make good on our previous deal."

"What deal is that?" I asked sadly. The energy level in the room had gone down, and Daddy's disposition had changed completely. The smirk he wore wasn't a good sign.

"You got Cat's bill to pay, remember?"

Every muscle in my body ached. *How could he*, I wondered. Didn't our relationship mean anything to him? When Daddy opened the door to leave, I followed behind, hoping he'd change his mind. However, there was a strange man standing outside my door dressed in a work jumpsuit with a tool belt strapped around his waist. He grinned like he was ready to put in work. I figured Ms. Dottie was playing me dirty, wanting me to get back to work so soon. But revenge seemed to be her style.

Instead, Daddy shut the door. The moment it closed, I heard loud drilling sounds. The screws went in quickly, and the new dead bolts, even quicker. I flung my body against the door, and screamed in agony. "Let me outta here!" I yelled. "Let me out!"

Chapter Twenty-Two

The heavy rain beating against my window-pane added dreariness to my already gloomy feeling. I leaned against the headboard, wondering how I'd gotten myself in such a crazy situation. I was supposed to work in the house for four months top, then be free, with enough money to make my way out west. But things didn't seem to be working in my favor. And to top it all off, being locked in my room was the furthest thing from my plan.

When I thought about how this all happened, *men* came to mind. They were the culprit. It seemed like every bad aspect of my life started from complications with a man. Me and my mom fell out because I started fucking with her male connection. Me and Rich weren't together 'cause he'd found out. And now I'd fucked up a good gig by catching feelings for the owner of a hoe house, who'd locked my ass up in my bedroom. *So much for escaping prison time.*

I hit myself in the forehead a few times thinking why, why, why? I'd be twenty-four years old in six months, so this craziness was getting old. I needed to grow up, make more mature decisions.

I hopped off the bed, trying to keep myself from going

insane. It was already noon, and no one had showed up to let me out. The day before, Ms. Dottie told me that she was finally gonna let me out. I hadn't been called down to the showroom, the office...nothing. I wasn't about to let it get me down, so for the next hour, I dropped down to the floor and had my gym time. I had to keep myself looking good, 'cause at some point, Daddy would come to his senses and understand that I'd never do anything to hurt him. Then we'd be together, for sure. That mess he was upset about was between me and my moms. *Not him.*

Time seemed to fly, and before I knew it, my work-out wasdone. I was extremely sweaty, so a quick shower and change of clothes was desperately needed. I'd gotten up extra early that morning, showered, and dressed like I was going to a party. I figured I could earn a few brownie points if I spruced things up a bit. Not to mention I had on Daddy's favorite outfit, a tight pair of True Religion jeans and a sheer cream shirt. Unfortunately for me, no one came by to see me looking good.

After my second long shower, and solo fashion show, four o'clock came and went. And so did more boredom. I needed another means of entertainment. Figuring out what to do next was mind boggling. Eating sounded good to me, but I guess Ms. Dottie's plan was to starve my ass to death, 'cause I hadn't eaten in two days. The only thing she'd managed to give me was water. *Even people on death row are treated better than this shit.* Luckily, the mints in my purse had provided some nutrients.

I made my way to the window, only to realize there were several cars in the driveway. I saw someone leaving the house, and I tried to get his attention by banging on the window. The gentleman just looked up, placed his hands in his pockets, and sped up his pace. I waved like a school-girl, but the client just nodded and hopped into his ride. At that moment, I realized no locks were on the windows. I could really break free if I wanted to. But where would I go? The situation confused me even more.

I held my head down low, knowing the client wouldn't be coming back for me. Then I thought of Tracey. If she were alive, I'd have a place to go. I just knew in my heart, my mother killed her. I couldn't prove it, but I'd bet my life on it.

Loud rumbling sounds outside my door startled me. My reflexes made me reach for the window. I guess I immediately thought about my break-in back in Jersey. As the noises grew louder, I became more frightened. As soon as I heard the locks being unlatched, my brain told me to hurry to the opposite side of the room, in search of a weapon. Unsure of who was on the other side, or what they had in store for me, I jetted across the room, and grabbed the small lamp from the coffee table.

When the door swung open, Ms. Dottie stood there a few seconds in silence, swinging her key ring. Her facial expression seemed to have pity on me. I geared up for a smart remark to come from her mouth.

"It's your phone time," she said, "C'mon down."

She turned away leaving the door wide open. I expected her to say, "I'm sorry, we forgot you were in here." Or, hell, what about breakfast, lunch, or even a fucking snack!"

These people are fucking crazy I thought, walking out of my room. Even though I'd finally been let out of my room, my pace was slow, and cautious. *Obviously anything goes around here.* Ms. Dottie reappeared and scared the shit outta of me. "Go eat first, you got some food waiting in the kitchen."

Okay…so maybe she did forget. She seemed to be off her game, which was different from the Ms. Dottie I was used to.

"Thanks," I mumbled. I didn't want to act like I was mad, but I didn't want her to think it was cool to have me locked up like an animal either.

After eating the old turkey and cheese with withered lettuce, I sluggishly headed toward the office for my phone time. When I approached the showroom, there were no familiar faces except School Teacher's. I waved, but she didn't wave back. I wondered if she knew I'd been locked up, or if she even cared. For that matter, did anybody care?

I kept it moving, hoping to run into Sushi. She had computer time right before me, so I hoped to see her. When I entered the office, to my surprise Ms. Dottie was right behind me. I thought she was gonna follow me inside, until she turned slightly and opened the front door. A tall gentleman entered. Ms. Dottie questioned him a bit, then ushered him into the showroom. From where I was sitting, I couldn't see his face that good, nor could I tell if he appeared to have money. His shoes were the only visible clues I had to say he was wack. The brown penny loafers were worn, and looked like the pair I wore in high school, literally.

I left the door to the office open, and logged in to my account on MySpace. After being locked in my room for all that time, the last thing I wanted was to be in a closed space. I really didn't know what my interest with MySpace was anymore since Tracey wasn't around for me to send messages to. I knew the messages and comments would've strictly come from people I didn't know. But, what the hell, there was nothing else for me to do.

My fingers starting typing fast, like I'd found some new-found energy. Once I logged in, I thought it was strange how there were a few messages from somebody named So-So- Special. There wasn't a picture, so I didn't have a clue as to who it was. I clicked the first message, then fell back in my chair. I took a few breaths and read the second message. *Oh, my God! It couldn't be.* I gazed deeper into the screen. It was him. The love of my life. The only man who ever loved me.

Candice. Hope you get this. I'm out, Ma. Been out for a couple of weeks. Your mother is out too. So be careful, watcha self. That bitch- BIG V, turned on me, wants to kill my mothufuckin ass now. I got your back though. Call me at same phone #. Rich

Just about the same time, my heart pounded from reading Rich's message, someone knocked on the front door. After Ms. Dottie opened the door and let the gentlemen in, I listened, hoping she would tell me the client wanted my services, but ironically the voice was familiar. An odd voice that I couldn't pin-point. At first Ms. Dottie talked to him about the policies of the house, then her conversation abruptly changed. She became defensive, so I scooted my chair closer to the door, still away from their view.

I peeked my head out the office door slightly to get a glance, and to see if I wanted to be bothered with the client's drama. Quickly, I snatched my head back. His face hadn't changed. Agent Barnes still looked like a lil' boy in his late teens instead of a grown man. Vomit built up in my stomach quicker than I could blink. Ms. Dottie got drilled with one question after another.

My whole face changed colors, wondering what the fuck Agent Barnes was doing at the house? I wanted to reach out and shut the office door slowly, but that move would've caused too much suspicion. Instead, I leaned back in the chair, trying to calm my nerves enough to listen in. I looked over at the screen where Rich's message stared me in the face. I was so distraught from Agent Barnes presence, I couldn't focus on anything else.

"I'm looking for Candice Holmes," he said firmly.

"No one here by that name," Ms. Dottie replied.

"She called me from a number here at this house," he said to Ms. Dottie.

"Must be some mistake," Ms. Dottie shot back.

"No, I'm confident. She left a message, and we tracked the phone number to this location."

I watched as Agent Barnes stepped a few more feet into the foyer, straining to get a glimpse of the place. I swung my chair back even further, hoping he wouldn't see me.

"Besides, we don't make mistakes," he said, flashing his badge.

Uh-oh, I thought.

Ms. Dottie played it cool. He must've disguised himself as a John to get past the gate originally. So now that he was in, she asked bluntly, "So what is it that you want, Agent? There's no Candice here."

"What about a Danielle Crouch?" he asked, looking around both sides of her shoulders.

"Nope," she said, without hesitation. Strangely, she wasn't as firm as usual.

"Well, what about the owner, James Woodruff aka Daddy? Or should I say whoever runs this place. They're gonna be in a lot of trouble if you don't wanna cooperate, so just point me in the right direction."

Ms. Dottie paused. "Yes, James Woodruff does own the place."

She turned to see if anybody was listening from behind. I'm not really sure if she remembered I was in the office. "What else do you need?" she asked, holding her hand toward the door. "I have nothing more to say."

"What kind of place is this exactly?" he asked. His focus was fixed on the chandelier.

"It's a group home for troubled girls," she replied, with confidence. "Check the city records. That's how we're listed. Licensed and all."

He laughed hysterically. Agent Barnes obviously wasn't buying it. I could feel it in my soul. I wondered if he had , or would just flash the search warrant I hoped he'd already obtained. I took in a quiet deep breath, waiting for his next move.

In a matter of seconds, he did an about face, and walked to the door. "I'll be back," he said, with a smirk.

As soon as the door closed, Ms. Dottie quickly walked into the office. She snatched the phone from the receiver and dialed. "Yeah, tell Daddy to get here as soon as he can."

"I swear, Ms. Dottie I didn't tell that man to come! I swear," I pleaded, as soon as she hung up.

"Meet me in your room," she ordered.

I wanted to respond to Rich's message, giving him the

address to the house, so he could come save my ass. Instead, I followed Ms. Dottie's instructions like a fool. My intuition said head straight out the front door. But by the time I got up to my room, I'd gained enough heart to make a run for it. I moved with speed toward the closet to grab my purse. I checked over my shoulder to make sure the bedroom door was still open. Then gathered what I could, ready to roll. When I turned back around, Ms. Dottie scared the shit outta me. She was standing in the doorway like Jason from Friday the 13th. All her ass needed was a fucking hockey mask. My eyes followed the length of her arm down to the huge chain she held. All I could think about was the time Daddy spoke of how he'd shackled a girl once. *Damn, how am I gonna get out of this shit?*

Chapter Twenty-Three

I stood out front of the address where my new connection said we'd meet. My instructions were to wait across the street away from the bowling alley on 118th Street in Harlem. That nigga sounded real sweet on the phone. I wondered how my daughter always found a way to get the good catch of the sea. Then I laughed. She got that shit from me. It was a skill we in the Holmes family was blessed wit. *We not only had the ability to get the ones we wanted, but also the ability to connive them dumb mufucka's outta anything our pretty little hearts desired.*

I sat on the hood of the car, waiting for that lying-ass mufucka to pull up. He said he'd be here in twenty minutes. The nigga didn't even tell me what he'd be ridin' up in, so my ass was scopin' every damn car that cruised by. Car after car I watched anxiously. All of a sudden a dark green Navigator drove by real slow. *Here this slow ass nigga is now,* I thought. I waited till the tip of the car got closer, then jumped down ready for bizness. The windows were dark as shit, so I placed my hand on my heat. One could never be too sure 'bout niggas these days.

As the window slowly came down, I was shocked. This little dark-ass nigga not even eighteen years old, asked my ass what the fuck was I doin' on his mufuckin' strip. Rich hopped out the car, 'cause his ass sensed it was some shit gettin' ready to pop off. I watched his little spook lookin' ass real close. I nodded to Rich.

"Your strip?" I asked.

"Yeah, my strip ol' head."

"Listen you little shi…." Before I could get the word out, Rich bust the driver's side window wide open with his Glock. When the lil' fuck went to shield his face, I ran up to the truck and shoved my piece down his throat.

"When I blow yo' shit off, yo' mama gon' feel it!"

He cried like the baby he was. "Uh…uh," he tried to speak.

"Shut the fuck up! School's in session. You just failed the first test! Don't you ever ask the teacher what the fuck she's doin'! You just follow instructions you lil' asshole."

Rich shot two rounds in his sideview mirror. We had to teach that lil' new school wanna-be dealer a serious lesson. Don't fuck wit yo' ancestors…yo' predecessors. I snatched my gun from his mouth and commenced to slappin' him across his face, like an abusive man beating the shit out of his wife. He clinched his left cheek like his skin was peeling off, which it was. Blood fell all over his cream Sean John hoody.

"Move the fuck on, son."

His lil' bitch ass took off like five-o was on his ass. Rich laughed and eased back in the driver's seat. There was no need for words, our motto spoke for itself- kick ass first and take names later. Wasn't no need for communication. That unnecessary shit pissed me off. It fucked my whole groove up.

I sat back on the hood wild'n out, 'cause the person I

needed to meet still hadn't rolled up.

I didn't realize for once in my life, how nervous I was until Rich blew the horn. I jumped up.

"You stupid ass, nigga. What the fuck do you want?" I shouted, tryin' to hold my composure.

Rich slipped his head out the window and flipped me his middle finger. I thought about walking over to him and yanking his fine ass out the car. Then beat his head in with my gun-split it down to the white meat just like I'd done to lil' Similac.

Luckily for him, a nice-ass Benz slowly turned the corner, and made me redirect my attention. I hated when niggas tried to be slick, but I was ready for whatever drama was comin' my way.

I repositioned myself further behind the car just in case I had to duck, or bust a few caps in somebody's ass.

The slower the car drove, I started feeling like it may have been that lil' nigga comin' back to retaliate. I pulled out my gun, this time exposin' it for all to see, and let it dangle by my side. The car stopped about ten feet away. I figured whoever it was, saw my shit, and knew I meant serious bizness. I didn't give a shit. I was prepared to let off some steel on somebody's ass. I motioned to Rich to stay put.

What had me more on edge was the fact that whoever it was had their arm hanging out the window in this cold ass weather. *Fuck it*, I thought. *No pain, no gain.* I took my chances. Strolling towards the Benz, I stretched my arms up in the air, as if to ask *what the fuck you want*. I locked my eyes on the car's every move until it pulled right up on me.

"Perfect timing," the fat mufucka said.

"Perfect? Check this Daddy, or whatever the fuck they call you. You call havin' me waitin' for thirty minutes perfect?"

I moved around to the driver's side, tucking my 9mm away in my spanxs. The spandex material was tighter than a mufucka, but it made my shape look good.

"So, where she at?" I asked, reaching into my back pocket.

He nodded, just studying me. Strangely this nigga looked familiar. I tracked my mental rolodex. I ain't want no shit. *Did I do deals with this nigga in the past? What the fuck! Maybe I fucked him? Was his ass a recovered crackhead? Damn!* I searched and searched. His smile…there was something about his smile. I let his ass talk a little more to see if anything he said would jog my memory.

"So, your next move?" he asked.

I tried to get him off task and used my ass as bait. He bit. I puckered my lips, and dropped my pen on the ground behind me. I shook my ass as seductively as I could. I turned back to see if he was watchin', and he was. He couldn't resist.

"I hope you like what you see." I smiled, showing him every tooth in my mouth. He needed to be mesmerized like all the others. I handed his ass the cash that was already bundled up in a fat rubber band. But he shot me a hand movement, like he was whisking the money away.

He undressed me with his stare. "Yo, you look real good. There's something real familiar about you. You sure we ain't been out before?"

Damn, that was it. I fucked this nigga! This nigga used to say this shit to me long before I ever gave his ass some, which was only once. "James!"

"What?" he said, lookin' baffled as hell. "You called me James."

I started snapping my fingers, like the snaps would help me remember. "James Woodruff. Yeah, nigga, that's it." He stuck his head out the window to get a closer peek. "James, it's me, Velma."

"Who would'a thought I'd ever see you again."

He stepped out the car, leaving the door wide open.

"Been a long time." With my arms outstretched, I gave him a big hug. I glanced over at Rich to see a dumb ass look on his face. I shrugged my shoulders. *Oh well*, I mouthed.

"You never called me after you gave me the good stuff. Damn, you still pretty as shit, but a lil' rougher now, huh?" He took a step back and searched me up and down. "Didn't tote a gun back then, wasn't takin'out muthfuckas either."

"Shit, that was over twenty years ago. Things don' changed. Now, it's all about survival in these streets."

"I see…I see. So, who is your friend," he asked.

"Oh, that's my sidekick. He cool," I reassured him.

"So back to business, sexy. You didn't say too much on the phone other than she told a lie on you that landed you in the penitentiary. So, you really wanna handle this little bitch, huh?"

I nodded with the meanest scowl possible.

"I'm ready, 'cause she been lying to my ass too," he said, like his feelings were hurt.

"Lying, huh?" I laughed. *That's her*, I thought.

"Yeah…and my house lady just told me she got the feds comin' to my spot. Now they hot on my ass. You doin' me a favor by taking care of her ass. So, where you know her from?"

This shit was becoming all too much for my ass. *Shut the fuck up*, I thought to myself. It was no time for getting emotional and shit. Nor was I gonna tell him she was my daughter.

"Uh…let's talk 'bout that later. I'm ready."

"Tell your little sidekick you ridin' with Big Daddy."

I sashayed over to the car, gettin' my switch on, and let Rich know that he could jet. He gave me the strangest look. I knew what it meant though. Rich was lettin' me know that he was comin' whether I liked it or not. Sometimes his ass thought he was my man and shit.

"Look, trust me on this one, it's cool. You go 'head and take the night off. I'm real familiar wit' this one." He stared at me as if he didn't trust me.

"A'ight. But hit me up if you need me," Rich responded.

"Cool," I said, headed back to James. I slid in his car all lady-like and shit as he looked over at me and smiled. Daddy pulled off like he'd just picked my ass up for a date. He reached for the radio, turning up the sounds of the Whispers.

"Cause you're my everything, all my hopes and dreams come true," he sang, as he winked at me. Little did he know, I felt like a piece of shit.

How in the fuck am I gonna tell him that the reason why I ain't never call his ass back is because he's Candice's father? I still ain't gonna tell his ass. How would that shit look anyway, both parents tryna kill their young? This shit is gettin' too deep.

Chapter Twenty-Four

After having my fifty second breakdown, I realized
Ms. Dottie must've been having a breakdown too. Her
eyes watered the more she glared into my face. "You
remind me so much of her," she said, clutching the thick
pair of iron shackles.

"Of who!" I shouted, in my most petrified voice. She
was scaring the living shit outta me, and I wanted out.
This was way too much.

The closer she moved toward me, I backed away even
more. When I took my next step, all I could think about
was how the both of us would die in this room.

"You think you special?" Ms. Dottie asked, with a
crazy look on her face.

"Look, I know you don't like me! Sushi told me what
you did! It wasn't Cat who fucked up my room. It was
you!"

Her calmness had disappeared. She screamed right
back at me. "I did it to protect you, stupid! I wanted you
to leave! I've done everything I could to make you leave!
But you just don't get it!"

I wanted her to stop talking in circles, 'cause none of
what she said made any sense. Finally, my frustration

ended with a possessed wild'n out session. Between the knocking sounds inside my head, and the shortness of breaths, I flung my arms high in the air, like I was fighting an imaginary person. I know Ms. Dottie thought there was no way to calm me down, by the way my body shook. For seconds, I moved around the room like a crack addict needing a hit.

"What do you want from me? Why are you doing this!" I shouted. I asked question after question, but Ms. Dottie had no answers.

Tears strolled down her face. The chains fell to the floor. "You think I want to do this to you?" she cried softly. "I grabbed this chain to show you what Daddy will do to you when he gets here."

My mind was so boggled, my face could only tighten. What in the hell was she talking about?

"You look so much like my daughter…Lisa. Spitting image," she added.

I froze. Her voice echoed around the room. Lisa…Lisa…Lisa was all I could think.

Her head nodded. "That's right," she confirmed. "That's the Lisa we've all been talking about. My Lisa." She held her palm to her chest, then began to sway fearfully back and forth. "That's why I can't do this anymore. I see it all happening again." Her eyes filled with regret. "She was my only daughter, sixteen when she first came here. We had no where else to go."

Instantly, Ms. Dottie fell to the floor on her knees. She sobbed uncontrollably, but my body wouldn't allow me to reach out and help her. She cried like a baby. I paced the floor for a few seconds, and then rushed over to the bed. I couldn't believe what I'd just heard.

"Why would you bring your daughter here?" I asked. She shook her head back and forth a few minutes, before struggling to her feet. "It wasn't a part of the plan. We were doing real bad when I met Daddy; living in a shelter actually. When he took us in, Lisa was only sixteen. She never did anything. I swear. Never even seen anyone have sex. But suddenly when she turned eighteen, she started dating Daddy right under my nose. There was nothing I could do. Lisa wanted to be with him," she said, with resentment in her voice. "Then, when Senator Marion met her, that was it. He fell for her too. She was beautiful just like you."

My face frowned. "You keep saying was. What happened to her?"

"Daddy let her go with Marion in exchange for him not shutting down the house, and bringing criminal charges against us. I was so afraid of going to jail. Plus, Marion claimed he wanted to be with her. I just assumed she was gonna be put up by him somewhere like a mistress, instead she never came back. The Senator says she ran away from him." Ms Dottie covered her mouth with her hands, and breathed a heavy sigh. "She's dead," she added, in the most horrified tone I'd heard in a while.

A lump formed in my throat. I didn't have a child, but heard there was nothing worse than losing someone you'd given birth to. Her next set of words, for some reason, made me think of slime, maggots, and dead corpses.

"Her body was identified a year ago somewhere outside of Philly," she informed me.

My heart skipped a beat. "Why didn't y'all turn the Senator in, if you think he had something to do with it?"

"I don't know, I don't know," she continued, as she

shook her head. "I think they do this to make money. The Senator has all kinds of connections and crooked friends in the world. I can't prove it, but I think they're selling girls overseas to the highest bidder, if they can trick the girls into going. Lisa probably fought it. Another girl went missing my first month here," she said softly.

"What?" I panicked. "Why did you stay this long?"

"I could never prove anything. Just knew it in my gut. Plus, Daddy has provided for me since he took me from my homeless state. I get one third of the profits from running the house…and he promised if he ever sold, half the house would be mine." Her head lowered. "But I feel like I've sold my soul to the devil."

"You have," I replied, in a whisper. "Me too, I guess."

"But no more…I won't stand by and see another young woman go down the drain. I'm tired of his lies!"

I sat on the bed with my hands cupped over my face, just listening, trying to understand why. I looked up at Ms. Dottie, then around the entire room.

"Daddy told me I was his woman," I finally said.

"Oh, yeah?" she responded, like it was all bullshit. "You're like a car to Daddy. He trades you all in for a new model every now in then." Her words hit me like a freight train going 100 mph. But I knew she was telling the truth. "Look at School Teacher. He messed with her mind too. He just lost interest in her once she went crazy. That's what he does," she pleaded. "Please understand that!"

I lifted my head a little to look into her face. Her tears had dried, and she now spoke with more confidence. More conviction.

"There's something magnetic about his ass that keeps

people wanting to be near him, no matter what he does. I just don't understand it, but it's true."

She paced the floor, like she needed me to focus on her lecture. I paid close attention, 'cause I was starting to believe every word.

"Look at me. We made an agreement after Lisa disappeared that he'd never sleep with anymore women in the house, or allow anyone to be with Senator Marion outside the house. I believed in that agreement strongly. He broke it! Prayerfully he didn't send Cat with the Senator too. She may be dead, or in another country by now. Leave now while you got a chance," she ended.

I felt lost, but I knew I had to run like hell. I thought about the money I sent out to a financial investment guy a few years ago when I was making money from my Columbian man. I couldn't get it until I turned twenty-four, but hell being homeless for six months would have to do for now. I hopped up thinking about what I was gonna take with me. I didn't have time to grab it all. Swiftly, I ran into the bathroom, then back out and into the closet. I grabbed what I could, then threw the covers back to grab my money that I'd stashed under the mattress.

A few minutes passed. I was so caught up in my escape, I hadn't noticed that Ms. Dottie had disappeared. I ran to the top of the staircase to check my surroundings, 'cause I wasn't sure who was in the house. It was a free day for some of the girls, but it seemed extremely quiet overall.

I jetted back into my room to grab some more stuff. I wanted this escape to be different from my last. I needed shoes on my feet, money in my pocket, and a ready-made wardrobe.

Ms. Dottie suddenly appeared at my door, wearing a black peacoat and a green knitted scarf. She held a small nylon bag in her hand, clutching it tightly as she spoke. "I'm leaving," she said. "You need to go now."

My eyes opened wide. *She was finally giving it all up,* I thought. I ran over to her and hugged her tightly. "Be safe," I said.

She touched my shoulder gently. "You too. Now hurry!"

Ms. Dottie turned and walked away. I went back to my last bit of packing. At that moment, I thought about something that needed to be done. Ms. Dottie was half-way down the staircase by the time I ran out with the necklace. "Here," I said. "Take it with you. It's a memory of your daughter."

She smiled, grabbed the necklace, and continued down the stairs. When the front door slammed, I knew this was it. It was time for me to be on the run again.

Chapter Twenty-Five

Fifteen minutes later, with my bags in hand, I took off down the stairs. The house was fairly dark, even spooky now that I heard about the scary shit going on in the house. Still in all, I kept my feet moving forward, ready to make my move. *The door- my future* was visible right in front of me. When I hit the bottom step, only three yards from my escape, I stopped like a confused fool, unable to make up my mind. Sushi's voice echoed from the show-room. It was a cheery voice, bad English at its best. A part of me just felt like I owed her a quick talk, to let her know what Daddy was really all about.

My change in plans was only temporary. Sushi, just needed to know. She'd been missing in action all day, but I couldn't leave without letting her know Candy was fin-ished. *Done with Daddy's House.* Truthfully, she needed to be out too; before it was too late. I wasn't sure how much she knew about Daddy, or his involvement with the Senator, but there wasn't enough time to compare stories. I took off in her direction leaving the front door behind me.

The sound of the door opening stopped me in my tracks. Sushi would have to be put on hold for a moment 'cause I figured Ms. Dottie had forgotten something. Surely she would fuss me out for taking so long to get out the house.

When the familiar smell hit the door, my hopes of an easy break-away went down the drain. His cologne seemed stronger than usual, but oddly still turned me on. When I turned to look over my shoulder, Daddy just stood there looking at me. His disapproval was evident. I wondered if the luggage in each hand signaled a dead give-away. I glanced down at the bags, then back at him. He returned the stare, to me first, then the bags. It was crazy. *Tic for tac*, I thought. He frowned at me. I frowned back at him. It was better to make Daddy think I was angry at him, for leaving me behind. I was ready to turn the tables and win the actress of the year award, until he spoke harshly.

"In there!" He pointed toward the showroom.

It wasn't optional. I could tell in his voice.

My heart beat like crazy. I couldn't tell him I was on my way out 'cause the look on his face showed he might pull some type of murderous stunt if I made one wrong move.

"I got an important customer," he belted out, following me into the showroom.

I moved slowly, giving Sushi the eye when I entered. Immediately, she knew something was wrong. He had a brutal look on his face as he nodded and pointed to School Teacher, Sushi, and Bambi. With each nod, he issued a snap. "Line up," he ordered.

I inhaled hard, like the breaths I took were needed to stay alive. I wondered if the Senator was the important client he was talking about, or if he planned on selling us off. "Daddy, can I run up and put on something a lil' more sexy?" I asked, in the most seductive voice I could muster.

My hands shook waiting for his response, but managed to point toward my cut up jeans and oversized polo hoping he would agree.

He walked in a three hundred and sixty degree circle around us as we all stood in the middle of the showroom floor. When he didn't even respond to my request, the answer was clear.

The other girls stood up straight shoulder to shoulder with their best faces groomed, and their sexiest stances ready. For them, they probably figured Daddy was angry, so it was time to make some money. In my heart, I knew differently, but I took my place at the end of the line like an idiot. I probably could've handled whatever Daddy planned on dishing out, until the unthinkable happened. The hairs on my eyebrows stood up when our important guest walked through the door.

"Candy baby, look who's back from the dead," Daddy teased.

I stood dumbfounded pretending I wasn't having a panic attack. I focused on the hip-hop attire my mother wore. The Roca Wear hoodie and extra tight jeans certainly wasn't made for a thirty-six year old. She always looked well below her age, but now she dressed the part. Even through her clothes the extra weight and muscles were evident. Her scowl was so hard…yet her skin and facial features remained eye-catching.

She immediately started at the beginning of our short line, never making eye contact with me down at the end.

"I never really liked Chinese food," she said, stopping

in front of Sushi. "That cat never taste too good. You cook cats?" She laughed like a crazy woman just before licking Sushi's cheek with her tongue.

"You funny as a mufucka," Daddy said, pulling over a chair to enjoy the entertainment.

"You think?" She never cracked a smile.

Her next move was to study School Teacher, who stood next to me. I guess Bambi didn't interest her too much.

"So James…"

Daddy's eyes lit up. "Daddy," he suggested.

"Whatever, nigga. So, now I understand what you told me on the ride over here. Yeah, these bitches can make somebody good money overseas. Especially this one. Lose the fuckin' glasses," she said, grabbing School Teacher by the crouch. Her powerful strokes made School Teacher turn a new shade, but she kept quiet, and my mother kept digging.

"I wish I could lick you like a lollipop," she said, as she continued to rub School Teacher's pussy through her pants. As Big V began to fondle School Teacher's breast, she let out a slight moan. "I'll be back for you later."

School Teacher looked completely humiliated as my mother continued down the line.

When my turn came, I tried to keep a straight face. She walked right up to me. "Ummmph…Look at my baby," she taunted. "Fineeeeeeee. All done up and shit. Look like you been gettin' money too. I taught you well."

My stomach did like twelve flips making me think I was on a roller coaster ride. This one moment of uncertainty was enough to give anyone a massive stroke. No one would ever understand my position 'cause it still didn't seem real to me. I squirmed, damn near pissing in my pants, yet this was my flesh and blood standing before me. When her finger reached toward my face, I jerked. But her movements continued.

"Look at yo scared ass. I taught you better than that. Man up!" she yelled. "At least stand your ground after you did all that damn snitchin'."

I didn't speak 'cause my guilt would be detected. All of a sudden she must've seen something on my skin, or felt something in her heart that made her facial expression change. I couldn't pin-point it, but there was something different. Her fingers clutched at my face softly, like a mother would caress her young daughter's skin. She tugged at my cheeks, which sent chills up my spine. I had no idea what was coming down the pipe. She looked over at Daddy, who sat not far away enjoying the show. He laughed in a low tone thinking it was all comical. I guess seeing a mother and daughter face off was priceless.

"Was you gonna sell her off too?" she turned to ask him.

He shrugged his shoulders, then crossed his legs not even worrying about her question.

"I know you said she was gon' be one of your best. I can see why."

"That's sweet Candy," he responded, then licked his lips in quick circles.

"Yeah…sweet Candy, huh?" she said.

"She too sweet to send off before doing her time here. Might keep her for myself," Daddy added.

Damn, my mother talked as if she was proud of me, proud to be my mother too. I even started to get false hopes standing there listening to her. Maybe we could for-

give each other, I thought. Start all over again? I wasn't
sure what would happen if I told the feds she wasn't
working with Luther, my Columbian connection. It was
me...*all me*. I was even the reason he cut my mother off
years ago.

I closed my eyes while my mother looked at Daddy
with curiosity in her eyes. There seemed to be so much
she wanted to know. It seemed like maybe she would give
me a second chance. This was the perfect and only
moment to repent for what I'd done. I reminisced back to
the day at the cemetery when I asked the Good Lord to
help me on my situation with Daddy. I promised that I
would pray if He let me outta that situation, and He did. It
was time for me to remember what my grandmother had
taught me about prayer. Not just for the moment, but from
here on out. I said a silent prayer asking for forgiveness
while my mother continued to question Daddy. Her voice
seemed to be distant, even though she spoke directly in
front of my face.

"You slept wit'er, didn't you?"

I opened my eyes to catch the tail end of his grin.

"You messed around with this fat mufucka," she
turned to ask me, but pointed at Daddy. "Tell me now!"

I nodded my confirmation.

"Against your will?" she questioned suspiciously. "Or
he took it?"

"Uhh...Uhh...I guess we sorta fell for each other." My
head lowered.

"You so fuckin' naive," she shot back. "Easy pussy."

She acted liked she was gonna hit me, so I flinched.

"He told me I was his woman." I did my best to sound
like the victim so she wouldn't beat my ass for being so

stupid.

"You planned on selling her off? Huh? Just like you did the other girls you bragged about on the way over here?"

My mother's voice trembled a little. She was so unpredictable. Maybe abusive men was her soft spot. Daddy could sense her emotions changing, so spoke up fast. "No......" he said.

"You don't lie too good," she snapped. Her face reddened.

"Nah...for real. She was a keeper. I was only gonna let her go with the Senator a few times. He's a good dude."

"You were gonna send my daughter with that maniac!"

"Your daughter? What the hell!" Daddy was so shocked he couldn't even process his thoughts anymore. "You...nev...never told me...she was...yo...your... daughter."

If I didn't know better, it seemed as if my mother wanted to cry all of a sudden. But she was too hard for that. If anything she'd cry on the inside. She'd rather die than to show her weakness.

She took two seconds to process all Daddy had said. Then rocked momentarily back and forth, showing she was in deep thought. My mother finally blurted out what weighed heavily on her mind. "You slept wit your daughter," she announced. "This is the child you fathered," she said in a whisper. "Our one night produced this. You fuckin' bastard," she added.

What the fuck did she mean? Them together? Me-their child? All the blood in my body must've rushed to my head when Big V snatched the gun from inside her pants, pointed it at Daddy's chest, and fired! Bang, was all I heard. One bullet in the perfect spot was all it took. He slumped over in his chair, fighting for his life, just as the deafening sound bounced off the wall, and sent the girls running for cover.

School Teacher hollered a long scream like she was running from a killer in a horror movie. She cupped her face and shouted as she ran for cover, "Ahhhhhhhhhhhhhhhh."

I tried to follow Sushi's get away route toward the front door 'cause I wanted to make a run for it too. I just couldn't break free from the gaze I had on Daddy's eyes…my father's eyes. They remained wide open with his black eye-ball rolling to the top of his lids. He clutched at his chest wanting to speak to me. But nothing would come out.

My mother's move took him by surprise, but not me. That was her style. She'd make you think you were cool-then she'd do you in. My face showed no shock, no expression at all, just the tears that flowed. I was steadily trying to do the math, wondering where the hell my father had been for the last twenty-three years, and why my mother never told me who he was.

"He never knew," she said bluntly, as she watched him squirm.

It was almost as if she read my mind.

"I never told the no-good-nigga. Just held my own." Her lip twitched as she spoke without remorse. "Niggas like that always say they not the daddy anyway."

She kept talking, but I could no longer hear. A bullet in my head was better than living with the fact that I'd fucked my father, fell in love, and snitched on my mother under false pretenses.

I cried out for the first time, as loud as I could. "We gotta help him!"

"Shut the fuck up! I didn't birth no fuckin' coward."

Daddy started gagging like he was taking his last breath. As a natural reaction, I jumped from my space to help him. I'd never seen anybody die right in front of me. I reached out to help the man who'd planned on selling me to Senator Marion. But my mother's pistol now pointed at me. I froze!

"Go 'head, take a chance."

Her pity for me had disappeared too quickly. I was starting to think she had split personalities. Then I figured, she was probably just as mixed up as me. After a few seconds, she started laughing at me crazily. Then a second later, she lunged at me. It took a moment for my mind to process that she had attacked me. The gun swayed back and forth, all across the top of my head. The bobbing and weaving, hopefully would save me 'cause one pull of the trigger, and I'd be dead. I fought hard, but my strength was pathetic compared to hers. Finally, she caught me with a right hook knocking me to the floor.

Luckily for me, I was able to pull her down with me. We tussled and rumbled on the floor like two wrestlers. I was hoping to get some help from the other two girls, but they were nowhere in sight. Finally, I knocked the gun from her hand, sending it clear across the room. The 9mm was a free agent- and the best woman would win.

My heart skipped a beat knowing I had a slight chance at living.

The odds of me getting out alive were seventy/thirty. *Seventy in my mother's favor.*

Even though she'd lost the gun, Big V still had me

pinned down.

"You a slick bitch. What'chu do wit' the money?" she shouted.

"What money?" I cried.

"You made plenty of mufuckin' money from that Columbian mufucka. Rich told me! You stashed it somewhere!"

"If I had money stashed, you think I would'a resorted to this?" I asked.

"You slick. I don't trust you as far as I can see you."

I struggled to lift my head in my father's direction. His breathing became heavier by the second; apparently dying a slow death. At that moment his breathing stopped completely. My father had taken his last breath.

I remained still for a moment. There was no escape obviously, and I couldn't even cry. I felt like I was on the set of some violent movie. This was war. Not just a family spat. My mother had me on the floor in a position where she could kill me. Suddenly, I heard the bones in my arm crack, while the pain zipped through my body. She had to have broken some shit. I didn't scream though, 'cause pain wasn't my concern.

Just then, a jar was thrown through the window, and the smell of gas filtered through my nose. When it landed on the floor, not even three feet away from us, we both fought like wrestlers going for the gold. We quickly scrambled on top of one another to get away from the rag that erupted in a small blaze. My eyes bulged when I saw that my mother's pant leg had caught on fire. Then from the corner of my eye, I saw another Molotov cocktail come bursting through another window. We were under attack from somebody on the outside, yet we fought each other for our lives on the inside.

My mother shook her leg like crazy trying to put the fire out, while I rushed across the room for the gun. She came after me, flames and all, but I managed to grab the gun. It felt heavy, cold, and perfect- all at the same time. I turned around and fired twice the moment my hand touched the trigger. My aim was low, lodging a bullet in each leg. I didn't want to kill the woman who gave me life. Surely if she had gotten the gun, I would be done. Death was the only thing good enough for my mother, but I just couldn't do it.

By now the flames had erupted higher and caught on to some of the furniture and structure of the house. We both coughed trying to see our way through the smoke-filled room. Big V could no longer walk, but she crawled like hell, bloody legs and all. When the smoke detectors sounded, I sped up the pace. Time was crucial.

I watched her scoot her way around the room looking for a way out. I dropped down on the floor on all fours and crawled over to my father, to confirm his death. I knew to stay low because between the rising temperature and the smoke the floor was the best place.

Sitting next to my father, I watched with tears in my eyes as the flames covered most of the lower part of Big V's body. I took a deep breath, hopped up, and headed toward the double doors of the showroom. When I began pulling them shut my mother called out from the floor. Her voice overshadowed the piercing sound of the smoke detectors. "Candice, just remember, when you do wrong, it comes back! That's my word!"

I shut the door anyway knowing she was right. Her face remained etched in my mind when I opened the front door of the house breathing fresh air into my lungs. Even though sirens were heard in the distance, I could still hear my mother scream loudly in agony, "Candice, always sleep wit' your eyes open!"

Chapter Twenty-Six

When I stepped out onto the landing, the sirens had gotten significantly closer. I was near being delirious, but knew the difference between fire truck sounds, ambulances, and police cars. Thankfully, they were all headed my way. From a distance, the flashing red and blue lights allowed a smile to slip through the side of my mouth. For the first time in my life, seeing the police was a good thing.

Somehow the gate was wide open at the end of the driveway, and three unmarked cars came scurrying up the hill. I moved as fast as I could down the stairs 'cause Daddy's house which I left behind was now engulfed in flames. I moved with a slight limp 'cause Big V had pretty much did some damage during our fight. My arm was either broken or sprained. I wasn't sure which, but it hurt like hell. For some reason, I was able to ignore the pain in my effort to get away.

When I reached the bottom of the step, near the shrubbery, surprisingly, I saw a familiar face standing off to the side with the evidence in her hand. My heart pounded. Would she throw the cocktail directly on me?

My quick prayer was answered when she winked at

me. I couldn't process why she would come back to help me. Or was Cat really helping me? Her purpose had me confused. She stood in a daze looking as if she was gonna throw another cocktail into the house. "Cat," I yelled out. "Don't do it!" I pointed to the undercover cars less than ten feet away from us.

She turned to see what looked like a slew of officers jumping from their cars, and three fire trucks proceeding loudly up the driveway. "It's over," I said to her.

"That muthafucka did me dirty," she cried out.

"I know all about it," I assured her. "Get rid of that shit. Hurry!"

She hurried over to Daddy's Benz and dropped the cocktail inside his car door, just as one of the officers ran toward me. It was Agent Barnes. He rushed past the other officers, waving his hand like I wouldn't recognize him. "Danielle Crouch," he shouted.

I just smiled, 'cause witness protection was some bullshit. It had been a while since he'd seen me, but my situation hadn't changed. I was still a problematic young woman, bringing drama wherever I laid my head.

"You're a hard-headed woman," he scolded, touching my arm with ease. "What happened to our little agreement?" he asked. "You should've contacted me the moment your identity was blown. I could've helped you."

I gave him a smirk thinking, *no you couldn't, no one could.*

"You see the moment I tracked you down, I brought help." He waved his hand in the direction of the many service vehicles surrounding the house. "Well maybe a little late," he said, looking at the burning house. He stood amazed with an expression that wanted to ask if I started the fire.

I turned away from him, glancing over at the fire trucks that had pulled up and parked in zig-zag positions all over the yard. I watched them in a daze while they rushed to pull the long water hoses from the back of the trucks.

One fireman, dashed up to me, and asked, "Who's inside."

I shrugged my shoulders.

"Was she in that house?" he asked Agent Barnes. He had such a worried look on his face, the fireman didn't wait for an answer. Within seconds, he led me to the back of the fire truck, and shoved an oxygen tube down my throat.

Sushi came running up the hill in a hysteric craze. She squeezed my face between her hands. She was invading my space, but I didn't even complain.

"The house!" she pointed. "Me so glad you safe, Candy."

Candice! I wanted to say.

"All girls out the house!"

"I think so Sushi."

"What 'bout Daddy?"

I shrugged my shoulders once again. "The firemen have already gone in to see who they can get out," I told her.

"Did you start this fire," Agent Barnes asked me once again, after talking to the Assistant Fire Chief now on the scene."

"No, I didn't," I said sadly.

I looked over at Cat who stood nervously on the side. "My mother did it," I spoke softly. "She was after Daddy, the man who owns this house."

"And you too, I'm sure," he added. "How did all this go down?"

I started explaining how Daddy showed up at the house with Big V not knowing she would try to kill me. I never told him Daddy was my father. I was too ashamed. Instead, I told him Daddy wasn't gonna let her shoot me, so she shot him, killed him dead. Then shot at me too.

"Are you gonna follow through and testify this time?" Agent Barnes asked.

I thought deeply about what he was asking me to do. Testifying against the woman who gave me life when I know she wasn't guilty was completely foul. My conscious told me to say no...I can't do it. But the sane part of me said, "Yes. I'll testify. No more running," I added.

My mother needed life. That would be the only way I could ever walk the streets of America. There may have been 50 states for me to choose from to hide. But none could save me from her wrath.

Suddenly, I watched two firemen escape the flames. The shortest of the two carried a body slumped over his shoulder. Instantly, the EMT workers ran to assist, and jumped in to do their job. The moment the others could see that the woman was alive, claps sounded. I recognized my mother's face and instantly felt defeated. Tears welled up in my eyes; not because they saved my mother, but because she was alive. I tried to ignore the fact that she put fear in my heart even being placed into the ambulance. I just stood there, turned away from the ambulance, and watched my latest home burn to the ground.

Epilogue

SIX MONTHS LATER

Six months later, I sat curbside in my rental car outside the Marshall Heights Banking Company with my eyes on my man. It was my twenty-fourth birthday, the most important day of my life. I'd been waiting over the past year to be eligible to collect my money. No one ever knew that I'd met Gary, an investment banker from Vegas back when I dated my Columbian connection.

Gary urged me to set up an account which was a trust fund for myself. The downside- I couldn't get the money until I turned twenty-four. I remember acting like giving him my $300,000 was the craziest thing in the world, but I now know it was the smartest. It was the only way to hide the money I was making in the streets.

"You going with me?" I turned to ask Rich.

"Nah… I'ma stay here and wait for you, beautiful."

He shot me his sexy-ass smile and grabbed a hold onto my thighs.

I was in la la land. I loved that nigga. Thankfully, I decided to call him a month after my father's house burned down to the ground. We hooked up a few months ago once I wrapped up all my business with Agent Barnes, 'cause I didn't wanna get Rich involved back into my mother's shit.

Even though Rich was still upset with me about cheating on him with Luther, he said he'd forgiven me. We've been like two peas in a pod ever since. His one request was that I didn't share any details about the sex life me and Luther shared. When I told him about the money I'd be getting today, he just said I was getting what I deserved. I told him what was mine was his, and we'd spend it together.

I leaned over, kissed him passionately in his mouth, then hopped out the car. He looked so sexy behind the wheel of our rented convertible Chrysler Sebring.

"I'll be back. You sure you don't wanna come?" I asked for the second time. "I told you I requested all cash. I might need help carrying all that heavy money," I joked.

"The way you handled your mother, I know you can handle this situation. When you come out that front door, I'll be waiting right here." He smiled, then blew squeaky sounding kisses through his lips.

I rushed off toward the building with a smirk on my face. It reminded me of the same smirk I wore a month ago when I walked out of the federal court building back in New York. I remember having enough courage to lie straight-faced right on the stand in front of my entire family. I told how my mother had the streets on lock, and how she was getting it all from Luther.

I couldn't believe the judge didn't show any remorse for my mother. Not even thinking about the fact that she'd suffered sixty degree burns and came to court looking like a burnt, crispy piece of bacon. He sentenced her ass to sixteen years on King Pen charges, conspiracy charges, and her most recent charge-the murder of my father.

I snapped from my thoughts as soon as I entered the financial institution. I promised myself I wouldn't let my mother's situation haunt me forever.

Before I knew it, I was thrown into some plush office, signed a few papers, and was handed a black nylon bag with the words Marshall Heights engraved on the side. Damn, this is how the rich folk do it, I thought.

Twenty minutes later, I pranced out of the building only to see my baby grinning from afar. I felt like a superstar as my chauffer continued blowing kisses. I opened up the back door and threw the bag in with a smile.

Like the race car driver, Mario Andretti, Rich zoomed off leaving the door wide open, and me standing on the curb. My mouth fell open as I waited to see if this was all a joke. Rich hit the corner at the light ahead, then turned to look at me with a smile.

I stood there looking stupid thinking about why Rich would do me dirty. Then I thought about my mother. She was right. I remember her saying it's a doggy dog world. When you do wrong-it comes back.

Every little girl dreams of meeting Prince Charming and living happily ever-after. But in the hood the Prince Charmings are ballers and we dream of living happily ever Rich! Now imagine being swept off your feet and upgraded from a nobody into a ghetto superstar. Imagine a life with nothing but the best things that money can buy. When Emerald met Dollar he quickly upgraded her into a overnight celebrity. Spoiling her with the hottest whips, the finest clothes, the fliest jewels and an unlimited cash allowance. Emerald represented a baller s chick to the fullest; she lived, breathed and swore by the hustlers anthem Ballin! The night Dollar asked Emerald to marry him; she knew all her blood, sweat and spit had paid off. She d be forever fly; Emerald knew the life of a baller s wife could only get more luxurious. But when a drop goes bad and Emerald's back is pushed against the wall. How much will she be willing to sacrifice to stay at the top?

Author website: www.nwhoodtales.com

Who Needs A Job When You're A Paper Doll

As a young girl Karen Whitaker dreamed of becoming rich and famous, promising to buy her mother that huge house on the hill with a Rolls Royce parked in the driveway. Her desire for material things turns into a grown woman's obsession with money, power and sex. Now of age, Karen possesses the brains of a scholar, beauty of a diamond, and a body that a Coca-Cola bottle would envy. She knows how to get what she wants even if it means taking advantage of those who trust her most. Greed and passion for tantalizing sex throttles her into compromising situations that may destroy her career and crumble her picture perfect relationship with a multi-millionaire. Take a journey into her intriguing story as demons from her past strike to unravel her fairytale life thread by thread. In the end, will she escape her dark clouds or be exposed as one money-hungry, conniving vixen?

Visit Nicolette Online @ www.myspace.com/paperdollthebook

Available At Borders, Waldenbooks and Independent Bookstores
Nationwide

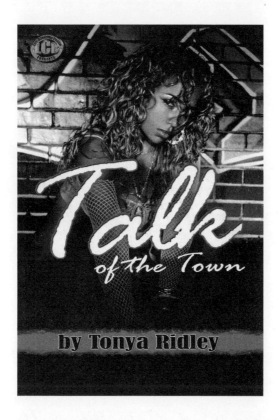

Diamond and Mya are best friends, who grew up in the one of the worst hoods in ATL. Both are determined to have it all, and soon become two of the dirty south's most notorious women. Getting money is their top priority, by robbing every hustler that crosses their path; but both women have different goals. Mya wants to be the next ghetto superstar. She results to sex and violence to reach her goal as she stalks every man with swollen pockets. Nothing will stand in her way of becoming the girl who runs ATL.

Diamond has dreams of owning her own hair salon, so she be-comes Mya's partner in crime, and makes the transition from stylist to thief; but their friendship will be put to the test when Diamond meets Scottie, a wealthy white boy, who becomes her next score. Diamond soon finds herself in a life of fast money and a world that takes no prisoners.

Lured by money and men, Still a Mistress explores the gritty world of good girls gone bad. A year after the tragic death of her family, Oshyn is still trying to piece together what's left of her life. While struggling to return to a drama free world, she is optimistic about her future. Little does she know that her cousin, Chloe, has reappeared to finish what she started, a vindictive cycle of mayhem.

When Chloe finds herself in water that's too deep, a face from her past comes back to haunt her. She ends up pulling out every trick in the book, determined to make it to the top. Get ready to enter a heart-pounding world of danger while Oshyn and Chloe take you on a ride, you'll never forget. Still a Mistress is sexually charged, and tests the boundaries of revenge when family vow to fight until death.

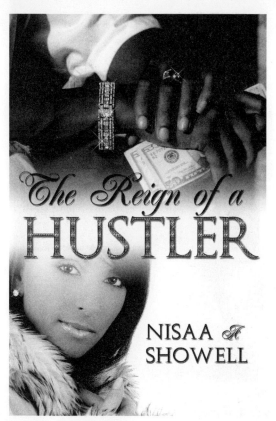

The Reign of a
HUSTLER

NISAA A.
SHOWELL

   The choice between love and life is never an easy one. Just ask Quinnzel "Supreme" Sharpe. Quinnzel has led anything but a charmed life. After shattering his knee in high school and ruining a chance at a college scholarship, his brother finances Quinnzel's way through school. But everything has a price. After graduating at the top of his class from Georgetown, Quinnzel takes his business degree and uses it to run his brother's drug dealing operation.

   Imani Heaven Best is everything Supreme has been looking for. She is Beyonce, Oprah, and Eve rolled up into one. Her business savvy, as well as her street smarts, makes her wifey material and she has his nose totally open. After losing her first love to the streets, Imani is not really feeling another ride down heartache lane. But there is just something about that man they call Supreme.

   Experience thug life and gangsta lovin' as a steamy connection ensues between two effervescently brilliant identities in this pictorial tale of raw urban hooks.

Drama is no stranger to Tiara James. With a mom on the verge of becoming an alcoholic and an alcoholic crack-addicted father who use to beat her mom in front of her, who could blame Tiara for finding a family on the streets. She lost people who she loved and trusted the most to death, jail or betrayal. From welfare, section 8, jail, drugs, abusive relationships and lies, Tiara's future seems uncertain. Brace yourself as Tiara James takes you on a rollercoaster ride in her footsteps, in her hood, telling her story.

Visit http://lashondadevaughn.page.tl/Home.htm

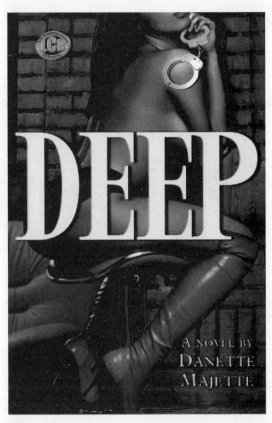

Money, Power, and Respect were the only things that mattered to Trae Keal. He was one of D.C.'s most notorious gangsters and loved the fact that there was nothing anyone could do to stop him from ruling the streets. The FBI knows taking Trae down won't be an easy task so they enlist the help of Carmen, an undercover agent sent to infiltrate Trae's crew by any means necessary.

Caught up in the drama with his new love Karina, Trae doesn't see his life unfolding in front of him. Unknowingly, he gives Carmen information about his operation that could send him away for years.

Once Carmen stumbles across a mysterious secret the FBI withheld connecting her to Trae, she finds herself in an uncompromising position that may turn the entire case cold.

Life Changing Books Titles

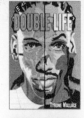

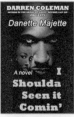

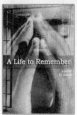

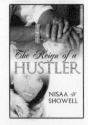

ORDER FORM

MAIL TO:
PO Box 423
Brandywine, MD 20613
301-362-6508

FAX TO:
301-579-9913

Date	
Phone	
E-mail	

Ship to:	
Address:	
City & State: Zip:	
Attention:	

Make all checks and Money Orders payable to: **Life Changing Books**

Qty.	ISBN	Title	Release Date	Price
	0-9741394-0-8	A Life to Remember by Azarel	08/2003	$ 15.00
	0-9741394-1-6	Double Life by Tyrone Wallace	11/2004	$ 15.00
	0-9741394-5-9	Nothin' Personal by Tyrone Wallace	07/2006	$ 15.00
	0-9741394-2-4	Bruised by Azarel	07/2005	$ 15.00
	0-9741394-7-5	Bruised 2: The Ultimate Revenge by Azarel	10/2006	$ 15.00
	0-9741394-3-2	Secrets of a Housewife by J. Tremble	02/2006	$ 15.00
	0-9724003-5-4	I Shoulda Seen it Comin' by Danette Majette	01/2006	$ 15.00
	0-9741394-4-0	The Take Over by Tonya Ridley	04/2006	$ 15.00
	0-9741394-6-7	The Millionaire Mistress by Tiphani	11/2006	$ 15.00
	1-934230-99-5	More Secrets More Lies J. Tremble	02/2007	$ 15.00
	1-934230-98-7	Young Assassin by Mike G	03/2007	$ 15.00
	1-934230-95-2	A Private Affair by Mike Warren	05/2007	$ 15.00
	1-934230-94-4	All That Glitters by Ericka M. Williams	07/2007	$ 15.00
	0-9774575-2-4	The Streets Love No One by R.L.	05/2007	$ 15.00
	0-9774575-0-8	A Lovely Murder Down South by Paul Johnson	06/2006	$ 15.00
	0-9791068-2-8	Changing My Shoes by T.T. Bridgeman	05/2007	$ 15.00
	1-934230-93-6	Deep by Danette Majette	07/2007	$ 15.00
	1-934230-96-0	Flexin' & Sexin by K'wan, Anna J. & Others	06/2007	$ 15.00
	1-934230-92-8	Talk of the Town by Tonya Ridley	07/2007	$15.00
	1-934230-89-8	Still a Mistress: The Saga Continues by Tiphani	11/2007	$15.00
	1-934230-91-X	Daddy's House by Azarel	11/2007	$15.00
	1-934230-87-1-	The Reign of a Hustler by Nissa A. Showell	11/2007	$15.00
	0-9741394-9-1	Teenage Bluez	01/2006	$10.99
	0-9741394-8-3	Teenage Bluez II	12/2006	$10.99
			Total for Books:	$

Shipping Charges (add $4.00 for 1-4 books*) $

Total Enclosed (add lines) $

For credit card orders and orders for over 25 books
please contact us @ orders@lifechangingbooks.net
(cheaper rates for COD orders)

*Shipping and Handling on 5-20 books
is $5.95. For 11 or more books, contact
us for shipping rates. 240.691.4343